Praise for Daisy Harris's
Nothing but Smoke

"Daisy Harris manages to present a story that is both incredibly sad and hopeful—and it is a story that no one should miss."

~ *Prism Book Alliance*

"This is a deep, emotional story that deals with grief, acceptance and finding happiness and a measure of peace."

~ *Fiction Vixen*

"This series continues to be really great and I am really looking forward to future books."

~ *Joyfully Jay*

"I have become a great fan of Daisy Harris' writing style. Quirky characters and humorous themes make for an entertaining read. In Nothing But Smoke, however, we are treated to a story with a bit more of an emotional punch and I liked it a lot."

~ *Smexy Books*

"...this book did have me in tears, and both Nicky and Michael were great characters, as much as this was a great story."

~ *Love Bytes Reviews*

Look for these titles by
Daisy Harris

Now Available:

David's Selfie

Fire and Rain
From the Ashes
After the Rain
Nothing but Smoke
November Rain

Nothing but Smoke

Daisy Harris

SAMHAIN
PUBLISHING

Samhain Publishing, Ltd.
11821 Mason Montgomery Road, 4B
Cincinnati, OH 45249
www.samhainpublishing.com

Editing by Sasha Knight
Cover by Kanaxa

First Samhain Publishing, Ltd. electronic publication: June 2014
First Samhain Publishing, Ltd. print publication: June 2015

Dedication

For my grandmothers.

Chapter One

Michael jogged the concrete path that wound around the reservoir in Seattle's Volunteer Park, looking up now and again for someone to blow him. He'd thought that by this point in the summer, it would have stopped raining. But as a lifelong Seattleite, he should have known better. Wetness coated the pavement and seeped into Michael's running shoes.

June-uary, the locals called it, though Michael had lived through enough of them not to be annoyed by the bad weather. More frustrating tonight was the lack of attractive men. Usually Volunteer Park was a great place to combine a workout with a casual hook-up, but no one so far had caught Michael's eye.

A few guys stood between cars at the end of the lot, talking and smoking and eating. Maybe the McDonald's bag perched in a bush near the group had been left by someone else, or maybe those guys had flung it in the most convenient direction, but Michael made sure to scoff loudly enough they'd hear him when he grabbed the garbage out of the greenery and went to throw it away.

Michael was still rubbing hand sanitizer on his palms when an engine revved near the park entrance and a guy on a motorcycle rolled in. Intrigued, Michael jogged in place as he watched the guy. Hardly anyone rode motorcycles in Seattle, especially during the rainy months. The drawbridges had metal grates that were terrifying to drive on when wet.

Leather Dude parked three spots from the closest car, as if he couldn't quite commit to staying. When he pulled off his helmet, curly dark hair framed his face. Maybe it was the motorcycle jacket, but he seemed broad. A daddy? Michael didn't think so. The way the guy hung his head, only peeking at the other guys, gave him away as one of those closeted straights who swung by the park for a quick suck before heading home to their wives or girlfriends.

Michael stretched his hamstrings as he watched the guy store his helmet. Leather Dude reminded Michael of his ex—the lying, asshole, closet case who broke Michael's heart.

Unfortunately, he also pushed every last one of Michael's buttons.

The guy was older, but not by much. Thirtyish, with wide shoulders, big hands, and legs like tree trunks under his worn jeans. He'd be perfect for a quickie.

"Hey." Michael walked over briskly, like he was just passing by on the way to continue his jog. "What's up?"

Leather Dude's cheeks were pink. Either from the ride or because he was blushing. *Cute.*

"Um, not much." Leather Dude got off his bike, though he hovered at the side like he might need to make a quick getaway. When he crossed his arms, his jacket creaked, releasing the smell of rawhide and engine grease. "Nice night."

"Yeah." Michael forced his breathing slower so he wouldn't seem winded. "Not too wet."

Leather Dude answered with a quirk of his lips, like he wanted to smile but couldn't quite do it. "Yeah. Hope it doesn't start drizzling by the time I'm ready to head home." He chuckled, jutting his chin toward his bike.

"Probably safer to ride when it's dry."

"Yeah." Leather Dude dragged his gaze down Michael's body, lingering at his groin for a second before starting his climb to Michael's face. He didn't meet Michael's eyes again, instead zeroing in on Michael's lips.

The guy swallowed, Adam's apple rising before bouncing back to its regular position. Leather Dude's neck was thick, ropey with muscles that disappeared under his collar.

"I was thinking of walking a lap as a cooldown." Michael tilted his head to the path. He watched Leather Dude closely, wondering if he'd get the hint.

"Yeah." The guy cleared his throat. "Yeah, me too." He crossed a few steps, not smiling, but Michael figured he knew what they'd agreed to.

"Great." Michael pivoted and started walking. Leather Dude was shorter and broad where Michael was lean.

"Um..." Leather Dude nodded at a wooded part of the trail where a few trees bunched together with enough privacy for a couple guys to get off.

"Looks good."

Leather Dude unfastened his belt as he walked. He rounded a tree to face the fence that surrounded the park. There were more trees beyond, guarding them from the flickering headlights on nearby roads.

He backed up, pants open and showing a gleaming pouch of tightie-whities.

For some reason, guys like him always wore the most boring underwear.

Michael pulled open the Velcro on his jogging shorts and shoved his hand down to grab his cock. He was hard already.

11

The fact that Leather Dude's bulge looked more than impressive only got him hotter.

"Oh." Leather Dude watched Michael's hand, eyes wide and nervous. He didn't move to take his pants down or reveal his dick. For a second, he looked so panicked Michael thought he'd back out.

"Here, let me help with that." Michael stepped so they were only a few inches apart. He stayed there a second, giving Leather Dude a chance to balk. When he didn't, Michael reached down, hovering his touch just beyond the jut of Leather Dude's dick.

Leather Dude arched forward, pressing his cock into Michael's palm.

He was hard. Thick. Made Michael think it had been way too long since his jaw had gotten a stretch.

"God." Leather Dude covered Michael's hand with his own, crushing his palm in tight.

He smelled like smoke and pine needles, with a rasp of musk underneath. It wasn't cologne or even aftershave. The scent was too clean for that. No, the guy just smelled great all on his own. His wife or girlfriend was a lucky woman.

Michael felt his way under Leather Dude's waistband. Precome smudged his palm, and crinkly hair tickled. Michael leaned in, testing the boundary of how close Leather Dude would let him get.

The guy tensed but didn't move away. If anything, Leather Dude's body seemed to light up, easing closer so his slick jacket brushed across the front of Michael's lightweight fleece.

His chest was solid muscle, heavy and warm and like Michael's dirtiest wet dreams. Michael put his mouth on the guy's neck. He didn't generally kiss his random park hook-ups, and for the most part they didn't want to kiss him either—but

Michael pressed his lips to Leather Dude's skin, wanting to taste some part of him besides his dick.

Leather Dude froze, hands on Michael's hips, gripping.

"You okay?" Michael wondered if the guy was on the verge of a breakdown. It didn't seem like it, though, since the cock in Michael's hand was still eager.

"No." Leather Dude jerked his head. There was a split second where his fingers dug into Michael hard enough to bruise.

In a quick move, Leather Dude pulled him closer, so their bodies pressed tight. He sucked on Michael's shoulder, his neck. He grabbed Michael's ass, like he was drowning and reaching for something to keep his head above water.

Nicky couldn't believe he was doing this again.

The gay guy was firm in his arms. Thin but wiry. He tasted so fucking good—a spicy mix of salt and sweat, cologne and male flesh. His short beard was clipped tight to his jaw in a scruff that rubbed Nicky's lips every time he got close to the guy's face.

He wouldn't kiss, though, no matter how much he wanted to.

"Damn." The guy had given up trying to jack Nicky off and ground their crotches together instead. Nicky's cock was out, sliding against the nylon material of the guy's underwear.

The guy worked his briefs off his hips, and Nicky felt the brush of something hot and hard against his cock.

He pushed the guy off.

"What?" The guy blinked at him. He didn't look angry, just confused.

Nicky had been playing this all wrong. "You know what I want." Acting a role he'd done more times than he wanted to admit, Nicky pushed down on the guy's shoulders.

There was a split second where the guy smirked. A headlight cut through the trees, and Nicky saw that he had blue eyes, and they were narrowed. "Give me your jacket."

"Why?" Nicky leaned against the tree. He felt awkward with his dick sticking out, so he covered it with one hand.

"The ground's wet."

The moss-covered dirt was waterlogged, true, but the guy was fucking with him. Unfortunately, Nicky liked it. "You should have brought knee pads."

The guy rolled his eyes. On another flicker of streetlights, Nicky realized the guy's hair was blond with a little red in it. Strawberry blond. No wonder he kept it in a buzz cut. If he grew it out and lost the beard, he'd be too pretty.

"I'm not kneeling on the wet ground. So either you give me your jacket, or I'll—"

"Fine." Nicky shrugged out of his leather and shoved it at the guy. "Now get down there."

Strawberry made sure the inside was facing up before folding to his knees.

Slowly, Nicky pulled his hand away.

"Mmm..." Strawberry licked his lips. He gripped Nicky at the root, pulling a stroke up the length of him. "Nice cock."

"Yeah?" Nicky preened from the flattery. Sure, he'd heard it before. But somehow it meant more coming from Strawberry. The kid looked like he was in his early-to-mid twenties, but he had the attitude of a guy much older. Nicky bet Strawberry didn't hand out compliments lightly. "You gonna suck it?"

Strawberry smiled up at him, clearly happy about Nicky talking dirty. He didn't break eye contact as he opened his mouth.

"Mmmmm..." Strawberry closed his eyes, humming as he worked his lips down.

All that warm wetness closed in on him, making Nicky forget about his mom's illness, or the guys at the station, even the shame of coming to the park in the first place. Nicky wanted to thrust into that space and forget every damn thing in his life.

Strawberry went at Nicky hard before pausing to lick around the cap. He was amazing, pretty as hell with his reddish-blond eyelashes fluttering. And he swallowed Nicky down like he loved it. Nicky thought about stubble under his lips...

No. That part had been an aberration. Nicky didn't kiss guys. Not even their necks.

Thank God he'd never see this kid again.

"Crap, it just keeps getting bigger." Strawberry jacked Nicky off with one hand, rubbing his own cock with the other.

Nicky's orgasm built, spreading through his body until he could feel it in his throat. "Shut up and do it." He bucked, pushing his cock through Strawberry's fist.

"Give me a sec to catch up." Strawberry sat back on his heels. He jerked himself and Nicky in time.

Closing his eyes, Nicky listened to Strawberry's panted breaths, the whisper of trees and the hum of the distant street. Every inch of his body was alive and throbbing.

None of the guys at the fire station would ever find out, not Father MacKenzie who came by to give his mom Communion since she was too sick to go to church, not the home healthcare aide who made sure his mom got her bath and took her meds on the days Nicky was at work...

It was just Nicky and this gorgeous boy at his feet, and Nicky was going to seize the moment for all it was worth.

He grabbed Strawberry's head. There wasn't enough hair to grip, so he cupped the back of his skull and pulled Strawberry's face to his dick.

Strawberry cursed around Nicky's cock, the sound a low-pitched groan. Nicky could tell by the way Strawberry shook that he was jacking himself for all he was worth.

"Yeah." Nicky thrust into his mouth. Wet, hot, tight. Slippery, because Strawberry didn't have time to swallow his spit. "Damn."

His cock tingled and buzzed, so sensitive he thought he'd go blind. Nicky bucked until his belly clenched.

Strawberry pulled off, gasping. "Oh fuck, oh fuck, oh fuck." He kept up his firm tugging on Nicky's dick. His scrunched face showed that he was coming too.

Nicky shot, the strand of white landing on the mossy ground. Strawberry pointed him to avoid his jacket, yanking spasm after spasm, until his hand was slick and Nicky was too sensitive for another touch.

"Oh, man." Nicky fell back against the tree, letting it support his weight. His legs shook, and the bark scraped his back, but that couldn't erase the wrung-out contentment coursing through him.

"Liked it, eh?" With a sidelong smirk, Strawberry shook come off his hands and stood.

Nicky reached in his back pocket for a handkerchief. "Here."

"Least you could do."

The kid took the cloth and rubbed it between his fingers before getting a small bottle of hand sanitizer out of his pocket to finish the job.

Laughing, Nicky accepted back his handkerchief. "You need a throat lozenge too?" He tried not to notice, but Strawberry was still half-hard, even when he was tucking himself into his shorts.

The kid would probably head off to find some other guy to blow him for a second round.

Nicky felt a pang of...something. All the shit he'd been thinking about came crashing down—how he shouldn't be at this park, and how he definitely shouldn't be letting guys go down on him. He should have been home, making sure his mom had eaten enough for dinner.

"I gotta go." Nicky pushed off the tree and buttoned his pants. He couldn't look at the kid, though those blue eyes danced in his memory.

"Yeah, I figured." Strawberry scoffed lightly—the sound halfway between amusement and disgust. "Well, see ya around."

Nicky wished he could say something to make it seem like he wasn't running away with his tail between his legs. He picked his jacket off the ground. It was still warm when he put it on, and smelled like forest and Strawberry's cologne.

He wanted to rib Strawberry about it. Who the hell wore cologne to go running? But Nicky was too chicken to say anything.

"Yeah, um... Have a nice night." Nicky wished he could hold the guy again, pull him into a hug. Maybe even give him a quick kiss goodbye.

The answer snapped into his head, like a whip cracking against his consciousness.

Leather Dude from the park. Fuck, fuck, fuck.

Michael dropped his gaze to his plate.

"Well, hurry up, or we'll be done by the time you get around to eating." Henri grabbed a chicken leg out of a bucket and headed to their spot.

Scooping casserole onto his plate, Michael snuck another glance at the man he'd blown in the park.

The guy's friends moved away from him, leaving him standing awkwardly on the outer edge of a conversation between a middle-aged man—who Michael figured was a boss of some kind—and a couple women.

Not that Michael cared, but he couldn't help wondering if the younger woman was the guy's girlfriend. He guessed not, since Leather Dude didn't lift his chin when she said something to him. Instead he kept his eyes on the grass like he was measuring its growth for a science experiment.

In the bright afternoon, Leather Dude's bulk was even more pronounced than it had been at the park. His shoulders and chest strained his shirt, his biceps so pumped they barely fit through the sleeves.

With a nervous scratch to the back of his neck, the guy darted his gaze Michael's direction before dropping it back to the grass.

What...? Oh!

Michael spun away, realizing the guy was ignoring him on purpose. God, that was weird. Normally when Michael ran into guys he'd messed around with, Michael was the one ducking behind trees or slipping into the nearest coffee shop to avoid conversation. He headed back to his friends before he was tempted to stare at the guy any longer. Something about Leather Dude had Michael wanting to twist around again, check out the guy one more time.

Blankets stretched out across the Beacon Hill field. Firefighters and their friends and families ate potato salad and grilled meat, while laughing with their kids. Henri and the others were at the east end, gathered on a blanket.

"Glad you finally joined us." Henri scooted closer to his brand-new boyfriend, Logan. Skinny despite his horrific diet, Henri didn't take up much space, but Logan was taller than Michael and had enough bulk to fill a good section of the blanket's surface area.

Michael should have brought one of the waterproof throws from his house. This was what happened when he let other people be in charge. "Don't worry about it." He waved at Logan, who seemed to be a really nice guy, despite being Henri's flavor of the season. "I'll sit on the grass."

He folded to cross-legged, managing to get a bite of casserole in his mouth before the dampness seeped into his hiking shorts. A few weeks into the sunny season, the ground should have been drier. The city must have watered the park some time recently. Talk about wasteful. Michael wished they'd let the grass go brown and save water.

"So who were you checking out over there?" Tomas, Jesse's boyfriend, bit a section off a chicken breast, smirking.

When Michael had taken Jesse under his wing at the coffee shop where they worked, Michael had figured the soft-spoken kid would be an easygoing friend. Michael hadn't counted on Jesse acquiring a winking Latino boyfriend who got off on rubbing Michael the wrong way.

"No one." Hell if he'd let his friends tease him about ogling an obviously straight dude. Some guys he'd known in undergrad enjoyed chasing unattainable men, but Michael refused to play that game. Closet cases were good for blowjobs. That's all.

"Yeah, right." Tomas tilted his chin, nodding in Leather Dude's direction. "I saw you looking. Pretty sure he works at the 13."

"Jeez, will you stop staring? You're going to give the guy a complex." Michael tried to keep his gaze on his food. Maybe it was Tomas's commentary, because Michael couldn't stop his attention from drifting to Leather Dude's body. Okay, fine, the guy might not have been someone he'd date, but Michael wondered if Leather Dude would be up for round two.

Tomas chuckled. "You should talk to him. He looks lonely." At the last bit, he snickered into his hand. "Maybe he needs a friend."

"Fuck you." Michael got on his knees and leaned across the group of them to grab a napkin out of the middle of the picnic blanket. He needed to get his mind off the fit of Leather Dude's cut-offs. "He's probably not even gay."

Oh, he might be a little same-sex oriented. Or somewhat bi. But Michael had been through all that before. Public conversations were reserved for guys who were fully and totally self-aware. Chasing the other type was a recipe for disaster.

"Not hungry?" The fire chief's wife's sister smiled at Nicky with a look of concern on her face.

Women were always doing that—giving him the sympathy smile. They didn't see that he could bench two twenty or that he'd carried a buddy out of a blaze the other day. All they saw was his mom's cancer.

"Uh, no." Nicky's stomach was too tied up from seeing that strawberry-haired kid to think about eating. "I should get home. See how my mom is doing."

"Oh, yeah. How is she?" The sister-in-law touched his arm, her skin soft and cool.

Her name was Becca, if Nicky remembered right. Blonde-haired, she'd been nice to him at last year's picnic too, and also at the station Christmas party.

The way her hand lingered on his forearm, Nicky wondered whether she was making a pass.

"She's doing okay. Finished up this round of chemo." Sometimes Nicky wished the whole station didn't know about his mother's battle with ovarian cancer. But when he'd had to take a second leave of absence to help her recover from a surgery, word had gotten around as to why he was missing work.

"Oh. So you opted for chemotherapy?" Becca made a face like she'd tasted something bitter. "I just don't understand how doctors can pretend that stuff works. It poisons the body. How can you heal someone by poisoning them?"

Nicky swallowed the bile rising in his throat. *Dammit to hell.* He heard this kind of crap from people constantly, but each and every time, rage boiled inside him so badly he wanted to hit something.

How could this woman stand there, smiling at him, and tell him that everything his mother had done to stay alive in the past four and a half years had been for nothing? Worse yet, how could she accuse Nicky of not having done everything he could to buy his mom more time?

"Umm..." Nicky looked in the ginger kid's direction, spotting him on a blanket with guys who must have been his friends. The only thing that got Nicky through the day lately was sneaking a few minutes of porn at night after he got his mom to bed. Now as Strawberry got up and headed to the bathrooms, Nicky's pulse kicked. If Nicky went over there, maybe they could... He didn't know what they could do, but at least Nicky could see the guy up close.

"Has she considered switching to the Paleo diet?" Becca batted her eyes, like what she was suggesting might actually be helpful.

"Listen... I should get going." He darted a glance across the field, hoping she'd think he was in a hurry to leave.

"Really? The party's just getting going."

"Yeah. But my mom..." His mother didn't really need him home, but the nice thing about having a sick parent was it always gave Nicky an excuse. "I need to check that she's taken all her meds. Sometimes she forgets."

The way Becca's forehead creased in a sympathy that didn't reach her mouth told Nicky she was only feigning interest. That was okay, Nicky was faking it too. "Tell Jack I said goodbye."

The squat, brick restroom building lay on the north end of the field, not far from where Nicky had parked his bike, and he rounded inside and washed the nervous sweat off his hands. He didn't know what he wanted to happen with Strawberry, but he needed to see him—maybe even smell him—if only for a second.

Bending over the sink, he kept his gaze in the mirror, watching for Strawberry to come out of the stall. A tall figure passed behind him, with a head of closely cropped reddish-blond hair. Nicky smiled in what felt like the first time in weeks.

"We've got to stop meeting like this." Strawberry leaned into his back, his whisper filled with teasing.

Nicky closed his eyes, letting the feeling of those words tingle to his toes. "Yeah," he said nervously. "Crazy, huh?"

A toilet flushed in another one of the stalls, making Nicky tense and pull away. *Shhhhhit*, Nicky mouthed more than hissed.

Strawberry smiled at him in the mirror, blue eyes sparkling like he knew Nicky was stressed out of his mind and thought it was funny.

The third guy in the bathroom came out to where Strawberry and Nicky were standing. He frowned at the two of them. "You guys done?"

"Uh, yeah. Sure." Nicky stepped over to the hand dryer. He should have walked out the door, but some irresistible force kept him in that cramped space, unable to look Strawberry's direction as he rubbed his hands under the blowing air.

"Thanks." Strawberry jostled Nicky away from the machine, but got between him and the door. There was a sly little smile on the edge of Strawberry's mouth, like he knew Nicky wished he could feel that touch again.

Unfortunately, the third guy stood there, crossing his arms impatiently as he waited to use the hand dryer. The set of his mouth made Nicky nervous, like the guy knew Nicky and Strawberry were flirting and wanted to put a stop to it.

"Excuse me." Nicky stepped around Strawberry and headed outside to the scalding sunlight.

Heart racing, he climbed the hill to where his bike stood sentinel from the parking lot. Halfway up, he spun to check whether Strawberry was following or whether he was walking the other direction back to his friends.

Strawberry stood outside the bathroom, watching Nicky leave. He didn't look away when Nicky caught him staring, just stood there, head cocked to the side like he couldn't figure out Nicky's deal.

Nicky waited for him to do something—wave or smile. Anything for Nicky to hold on to for his long nights alone.

Strawberry cupped a hand to his mouth and called up the hill. "Later?"

Before Nicky could figure out what he was agreeing to, he was nodding.

With a pinch of his mouth that may have been a smirk or a smile, Strawberry nodded back before returning to the picnic.

Chapter Three

"I'm home!" Nicky called into the living room as he threw his jacket at the bench by the door.

The sound of his mother's favorite program filled the house, but the volume lowered. "Nicky? Is that you?"

The air inside was stifling. "Yeah. It's me." He plucked at the front of his shirt, billowing air to his damp armpits. "Hey, are you drinking enough liquids? It's hot in here."

In the living room, his mother sat on the couch. Her feet were propped on the coffee table, and she was wrapped in a quilt, clutching a rosary in one hand and a remote in the other. She wore a beanie over her thin hair, making her look like a younger version of herself. "Yes, dear." She gestured at her cup on the coffee table. There was tea inside, but since Father MacKenzie had been by earlier in the day, Nicky suspected her drink had been tipped with her favorite flavor of schnapps.

Strictly speaking, his mom shouldn't have the stuff, but the good Father liked to spoil her, sneaking in her favorite chocolates from See's even though they did a number on her digestion. The nurses at the hospital might frown on her breaking her diet plan. Worse, Nicky might feel guilty for letting it happen. He had to admit his mom was right, though, there was no point in surviving this long if she couldn't have a little fun.

"Did you have a nice time at the barbecue earlier?" she called to him.

He went into the kitchen to pour her something that wouldn't dehydrate her, and returned to the living room.

"Yeah." Nicky set the glass next to her other cup and placed two pills beside it. His mother was supposed to take Marinol to increase her appetite, but she tended to forget. "It was nice to see the guys."

The sound of televised mass carried through the living room. "Lord be with you..."

His mom replied under her breath, "And also with you..."

The greeting on this show was her favorite, since this was the only mass on television that still used the missal from before they changed it in 2011.

So when the priest continued, "Lift up our hearts," Nicky replied along with his mother, "We lift them up to the Lord."

"Let us give thanks to the Lord our God."

Nicky caught his mother's smile as they said in unison, "It is right to give Him thanks and praise."

More and more when his mother watched regular television shows, her face would tense. Nicky knew she couldn't always understand the storylines, and was too embarrassed to ask him or her home health aide to explain.

However, this mass program was the same every time, the words a recital Nicky had heard every Sunday growing up. He could tell by the way his mom's muscles relaxed, her face settling into an expression not unlike meditation, that watching it gave her at least as much comfort as her pain pills.

The priest launched into the rest of the prayers, so Nicky eased his way toward the door. Not that he minded watching mass with his mother, but he needed to do some chores before heading to the gym. "I'm going upstairs for a bit."

"Okay." His mother's attention was back on the screen. Absentmindedly, she waved a tired hand at him. "Did you meet any nice girls at the party?"

"Yeah. Sort of." Becca's words still bugged him, but he knew she hadn't meant anything by them. Anyway, there was no harm in spinning a story his mother might like to hear. "The fire chief's sister-in-law seems nice enough."

The corners of his mother's eyes, which were so often crinkled with pain, softened. "That's good. Maybe you can take her out sometime." Her expression became dreamy, unfocused. She might have been thinking about catching a daughter-in-law, or she might be having one of her tricks of memory where she thought Nicky was a teenager again. Either way, she was happy, so Nicky didn't question it.

"Yeah, maybe." Nicky jogged up his stairs to his room. After tossing his sweaty clothes in his laundry basket, he grabbed fresh shorts and a tank top out of his drawers. "You need laundry done?" he shouted down the stairs, but when his mom didn't answer, he cracked her door and added the contents of her laundry basket to his own.

Jesus stared from a painting behind her bed, crown of thorns digging painfully into his scalp. His hand was raised like he was saying, "Yo."

Nicky needed to get out of there before he starting thinking about the expressions on all the statues in his mother's cluttered room.

In the downstairs hallway, he loaded their clothes in the wash. Then he hurried to the door, not wanting her to see him in his workout clothes. Even in summer, she'd always insisted he wear long shorts, as if flashing some thigh was akin to being naked. "I'm going to head to the gym for a couple hours. Do you need anything?"

"What did you say the name was of the girl you like?"

Nicky rubbed the back of his neck, and his fingertips met scalded skin. Damn place between his motorcycle helmet and his jacket always got sunburned when he rode. "Becca." His mom would never meet the girl, so it didn't seem to matter. "I forgot to ask, do you need help going to the bathroom?"

He'd only had to help her with that a few times, but he always worried she wouldn't admit if she needed it.

"No. I'm fine, Nicky. Don't worry."

Nicky nodded to himself, reaching for the doorknob. He skipped grabbing a jacket, since he'd be walking to the gym. "Okay, then. See you later."

Six hours later—after working out, returning home to change clothes and heading to the park—Nicky pulled into a parking spot, where he got off his bike. Nearby, a couple guys leaned against a car eating from a takeout container. One must have said something funny, because the other laughed.

Nicky's chest ached, though he wasn't sure why.

Maybe because this whole thing was depressing—coming to the park hoping strawberry-haired guy had been serious. But Nicky couldn't ride home to his empty room in his mother's dark house. He needed this tonight. To feel like another human being understood him, if only for a few minutes.

"Hey." Strawberry walked up. His green fleece jacket looked good with his eyes—made them more aqua than blue. His jeans and hiking sandals were low-key enough that if they weren't at a park in a gay neighborhood, Nicky wouldn't have necessarily thought there was anything *off* about him.

"Yeah. Hi." Nicky had no idea what to say, but any chance Strawberry would believe Nicky had only hooked up with a man that one time went up in smoke. Strawberry would know. Fuck, he knew already. Nicky was an idiot. "Um...nice seeing you this afternoon."

Strawberry cocked his head to the side, a smile spreading slowly across his face. "Yeah. So, you're a firefighter, huh?"

Nicky swallowed against a lump in his throat. "Yeah. And you?"

"I'm in school. At the U. Finished undergrad in May and starting a masters in sociology in September. My area is Stratification, Race and Ethnicity."

Nicky licked his lips nervously. He hardly knew what sociology was, and had nothing interesting to say about it. Instead, he settled for the basics. "Cool. I'm Nicky."

"Michael." Strawberry crossed his arms.

Tongue-tied, Nicky tried to figure out what came next. The night they'd hooked up before had been easier. Nicky just followed where Michael had led. This—was it seduction? A date? Nicky didn't even know what to call it, but his mouth refused to move.

An SUV pulled into the lot, and on reflex Nicky spun away so the driver wouldn't be able to make out his face.

"Nice." Michael's eyes narrowed. That sneer made Nicky feel ten times worse than the stupid SUV full of strangers. "So, are we going to do this or what?" Michael crossed to the path around the reservoir.

"Sorry," Nicky mumbled as he fell into step behind.

"Whatever." Michael kept up his quick-paced walk until he got to approximately the same spot where they'd made out a few weeks ago. "There?" Michael jerked his head toward the trees. He caught Nicky's hand.

Something that felt like joy coursed through Nicky, tinged with enough adrenaline to make him want to sprint away from their spot. His attention landed on their clasped hands, and how—although they were still on the path around the reservoir—Michael didn't let go.

Michael stepped closer. Close enough there was only a half foot of space between them.

"I can't do this out here," Nicky murmured.

The way Michael's eyes sparkled, he must have known Nicky was uncomfortable. Worse, Michael nibbled his bottom lip like he thought it was funny. "Okay. But what do you want to do in there?"

Nicky tried to regain his footing. The challenge in Michael's eyes made his chest flare with heat. With a pass of his fingertip, he touched Michael's lips. "This?"

Michael tipped his head back, smirking. "No thanks."

Nicky's mind raced. "I'd be up for a hand job instead."

"Hmm." Michael's smile spread like he'd just scored a point. "I could use one myself. How about we trade?"

"Uh...I guess." Nicky's mind blanked out, all his blood rushing to the solid pike in his pants as Michael led him between the trees.

Michael got a hand on the bark next to Nicky's head, backing Nicky into a large cedar. Michael stared into Nicky's eyes like he could dig out every last one of Nicky's secrets with a dull machete and leave Nicky bleeding on the ground.

"Get away from me," Nicky said, not as forcefully as he meant it, especially since his dick was stiff and Michael probably felt it against his hip.

"Thought you said you wanted a hand job." Michael's lips were so close, wet and pink. He roamed his fingers down Nicky's arm and dragged Nicky's hand to his crotch. *Oh my Lord.* Michael was hard under there.

Nicky grabbed Michael by the front of his jacket, meaning to push Michael away. Instead, Nicky yanked Michael closer.

Michael smelled woodsy and clean but with the sharp edge of some kind of cologne. Funny he wore it. Polar-fleece-wearing guy like him seemed like the kind to hate perfume.

"I'm not unzipping anything until you do," Michael breathed in his ear. His lips teased Nicky's neck, and he toyed with Nicky's fly. As promised, Michael didn't pull it down.

Nicky fumbled his way along denim, searching for the sharp metal of a zipper and finding only buttons. Sparse belly hairs tickled his fingertips.

"Yeah," Michael whispered, his lips tracing the shell of Nicky's ear, his breath roaming into Nicky's hair. "Like that."

Nicky popped open the buttons. Right there, demanding attention, was Michael's cock. It was narrow, but longer than Nicky's, as evidenced by the cap threatening to push right past Michael's waistband.

He maneuvered his way into Michael's underwear, feeling warm and humid skin and crinkly hair. Then there was nothing but a heated shaft, seemingly made for Nicky's grip.

Michael was going to kiss him. Nicky jerked his head back, but only managed to scrape his scalp on the tree.

With a slant of his head, Michael's lips were on him—hard and rough with stubble around the edges. When Michael pressed his tongue inside, Nicky wanted to growl, but he wasn't sure whether he'd be doing it in anger or pleasure.

In a rush, Michael got Nicky's cock out. For a second, Michael's prick brushed against Nicky's like a wet, hot, lick. Then Michael took them both in his long-fingered fist.

For the space of a dozen strokes, Nicky closed his eyes and went with it, his attention laser focused on the too-good feeling of them crushed together, but then Michael reached into his pocket and pulled out a packet of something, and Nicky grabbed Michael's wrist. "What the hell is that?"

"For fuck's sake." Michael bit open the perforated top. "I'm just getting my hand wet." He squeezed jelly into his palm, chuckling a little at Nicky. "You gonna let go?" Michael cocked his eyebrows.

"Fine." Nicky leaned back against the tree, his dick sticking straight forward. Fuck it. He was doing this. Wherever it led. Nicky needed Michael's hand on him worse than he'd needed anything in a long time.

He closed his eyes. "Yeah, sounds good."

Nicky looked like a live wire. Excited, rough and strong. For some reason, he let Michael take the lead, which had Michael a little confused and yet more turned on than he could remember.

"Good, right?" The lube was warm from his pocket, and it felt like sinking into a mouth.

"Oh God...fuck." Nicky clutched him by the neck of his jacket and pulled him closer. This time when they kissed, it was Nicky dragging Michael in tight, moving under Michael's mouth.

Michael wouldn't have been surprised if Nicky had shoved Michael off when he went in for the kill. But it had been so damn long since Michael had tangled tongues with any man.

He'd forgotten how much he loved the feel of breath on his lips. Better still was the desperate way Nicky kissed—lips hard and rough, his teeth scraping. For the first time since they'd started, Michael felt how powerful Nicky was—strong enough to throw Michael against a tree if he wanted. That made Nicky letting Michael drive all the sweeter.

Nicky rocked into Michael's hand, his cap rubbing Michael's in a steady *click, click, click*. When Nicky gasped, his cock spewed wetness all over Michael's hand, and the slippery perfection made Michael crazy. He panted, his voice getting higher pitched since he was close. "Oh God." He wished he were the one leaning against the tree, since his legs were shaking.

Nicky spun Michael so his back hit the bark, and slapped Michael's hand away to jerk him with desperate pulls.

Though Michael's impending orgasm vibrated from his toes to his scalp, his mind rebelled. It shouldn't feel this good...hadn't felt this good since Mark.

"Come on." Nicky tilted his head to the side like he wondered why Michael couldn't come. Leaning in slowly, Nicky only closed his eyes at the last minute.

His lips were soft, and careful. So different from the rough way he worked Michael's cock. Against Michael's mouth, Nicky said, "It's okay."

Michael could have cried, that was how hard the orgasm hit. The spasms wrenched from deep in his guts, places he hadn't reached for a long time, and he curled into Nicky's arms. He had Nicky by the shoulders, his face in Nicky's neck. Michael wished he could let go.

"You okay?" Nicky said.

"Oh, um, yeah." Michael rubbed his nose on the back of his forearm. God, he had to get it together. "Dry weather is hell on my allergies."

He pulled a packet of tissues out of his pocket and handed a couple to Nicky. Since he couldn't meet Nicky's eyes, Michael kept his attention on what he was doing as he tucked himself into his pants.

"Yeah. Me too." Nicky checked Michael's expression. "Uh, thanks. That was good."

"Yeah." What was Michael supposed to say to a guy who'd just rocked his world but he couldn't imagine seeing again? "You too." He darted a glance between the trees to the reservoir. "You want to head out?"

"Yeah." Nicky walked ahead, over the spongy ground and back to the concrete of the pavement. Another couple guys were fifty yards past and heading into the woods.

Michael felt empty, like a giant hole of need had opened up and he had nothing to fill it. Damn Nicky for stirring up those thoughts about Mark. In the woods, it was like Michael knew Nicky, but in the bright halogens of the reservoir, Michael saw their hook-up for what it was—nothing important.

They got to the parking lot and passed Michael's car, and Michael figured it would be the end of their interaction. He wished that didn't make him sad. "This is me." He gave the Mustang a halfhearted wave.

"Ooh, nice." Nicky's eyes lit up. "I haven't seen one of these in years." He ran a reverent hand over the rust-streaked hood. "It's a classic. Is the color custom? I've never seen one in purple."

The rush of warmth spread through Michael's chest that someone had finally—*finally*—recognized the value of the machine he'd worked to keep running for five years. "I think it was custom. At least, that's what the guy who gave it to me said."

"I know a guy who restores classic cars like this. He goes to my gym." Nicky kept his attention on the car, but the pinch of his lips said he was casting a line and hoping Michael took a bite. "You wanna trade phone numbers? I could, uh, get his info for you."

"Huh." Michael never would have guessed Nicky would try and maintain contact, and that's what Nicky was doing. After all, a Google search would give Michael the names of dozens of mechanics. "You serious?"

"Yeah. Why not?" The tension of Nicky's shoulders said that his certainty was tenuous.

"Don't take this the wrong way, but I wouldn't have thought you were *out*." Michael scanned over Nicky's clothes, from his worn sneakers past his brightly colored workout pants, and to his T-shirt with the cut-off sleeves. Nicky's leather jacket lay across his motorcycle seat.

Michael didn't pay much attention to fashion, preferring to shop for brands that were sweatshop-free and made of renewable materials, but Nicky looked like he'd just walked off a Bowflex ad.

"No. I'm not." Nicky's voice lowered an octave. "But we could meet up again..." He darted his gaze to Michael's crotch, and his eyes went dark and hopeful.

The hole in Michael's chest stretched wide enough to crack the pavement and suck him into the earth. "I don't date guys who can't be open in public."

"Well, uh...okay." Nicky frowned at the sidewalk.

"Yeah. Sorry." Michael had no idea why guilt was plucking at his insides. Damn Nicky and those wide eyes of his. They were big and brown—round, with thick, almost swollen bottom lids—and totally out of place on a guy so ripped. Despite his better judgment and everything Michael knew was in his best interest, he pulled out his phone. "But my car's been on the fritz a lot lately, so if it was just to get the mechanic's number..."

Nicky's smile lifted his cheeks. "Yeah. Yeah, just so I can call with the guy's number. I mean there can't be too many people who know what they're doing with your kind of car." Nicky bounced on the balls of his feet. "I'm two-oh-six, five-five-five, three-eight-oh-seven."

Michael typed in the number and let it ring until Nicky's voicemail activated. That way Nicky would have Michael's number too. "Okay?" Michael's nerves strung tight until he felt a tension headache gathering under his scalp. He shouldn't have shared his number. This guy could be a psycho, or a stalker. Or worse, a guy who wanted to see Michael on the side, keeping it some big, hairy secret until Michael was left sobbing manly tears into his pillow.

"So, call me with the number. If you want."

"Yeah." Nicky rubbed the back of his neck. "Soon as I run into him again. I have to work tomorrow."

Michael nodded. "Yeah, well, whenever."

"Yeah." Brown eyes searched, roaming all over Michael's body like they were looking for some answer to a question. "Bye."

"See ya." Michael unlocked his car and slid into the front seat.

When his engine coughed to life and cooperated enough to get him rolling out of the park, Michael glanced at Nicky in his rearview mirror.

Nicky hadn't left his spot on the sidewalk. Maybe Michael imagined it, but Nicky swiped his hand like he was making the sign of the cross.

Feeling guilty about what they'd done? Or hoping they'd do it again?

Michael shouldn't be getting involved with a guy still in the closet. He'd be thinking about that stupid gesture all night, trying to figure out what it meant.

Chapter Four

Nicky wished he could have gone to the gym and gotten the number for Michael the next day, but since his twenty-four-hour shift started at eight a.m., he didn't have time to think about Michael much less come up with an excuse to call him. All day, he ran between building inspections, training sessions and a car accident that thankfully had no casualties. As evening closed in, he was in a bunk in the firehouse, resting his eyes for a few minutes, so he'd be fresh if he had to go out on a call.

His phone rang like a siren under his fingers—the ringtone he'd set for his mother.

Nicky tensed before he even answered. "Mom?" His mother never called when he was at work.

"Nicky?" She paused to take a labored breath, as if she could barely get in enough air to talk. Instead of speaking, she coughed in a wet hack.

"Shit, Mom." Panic washed away his guilt over cursing. "Don't worry about talking, okay. I'm on my way home." He kicked out of his bunk and dropped to his feet. "You just have to tell me one thing."

"Mm-hmm?" His mother coughed more softly.

"Do you need me to call an ambulance?" God, those were expensive. His mother had needed one after her second surgery when she'd developed pneumonia. Nicky hoped like hell she didn't have that again.

"No." Her breathing was a little calmer now. Labored, but not gasping. "Just, come home."

"Yeah." Nicky tucked the phone under his ear as he rushed out of his station uniform and into his regular clothes. He shoved into his shoes, trying to catch his boss's eye, since Hank was busy with Cody by the truck. "I'll be home in five minutes, okay? Set your clock if you want."

His mother said "Mm-hmm" again, like she didn't dare speak or she'd cough.

"Be right there." Nicky clicked off the phone.

As he strode in his boss's direction, Hank looked up. His quick frown and the slump of his shoulders said that he knew what Nicky was coming over to say. "What's going on?"

Nicky hated having to leave work. With how many personal days he'd already taken, his leave bank was nearly empty. "My mom's sick again. She needs to go to the hospital. I'm..." God, he hoped like hell his boss didn't make a big deal out of it. "I'm sorry, but I've gotta go."

Hank nodded. "I know." There was a pinch in his lips that said Hank wanted to say something more. Probably that Nicky's mother needed more than just Nicky and a couple-hours-a-day nurse to look after her.

"Thanks." Whatever his boss thought of him at that moment, Nicky couldn't worry about it.

Outside, he kicked over his bike. In a hurry, he didn't bother with a helmet as he rushed to pull his bike across the sidewalk to the road.

"Motherfucker!" A cyclist screeched to a halt, slamming into Nicky's side. His messenger bag flew over his head and clocked

Nicky in the face. But the kid himself scrabbled away, hopping off his bike.

"Ow!" Nicky grabbed his cheek. Glad as he was that he hadn't hit the kid, he grimaced at the feel of wetness in his hand. "You okay? I'm sorry."

Desperately, Nicky tried to help the kid while keeping balance. But even with his feet planted firmly on the ground, Nicky wobbled.

"Asshole!" The cyclist gave him a shove, almost knocking Nicky off the bike. The kid must not have been too badly hurt because he threw a leg over his saddle and rode off. "Fuck you!" he shouted, giving the finger as he rode away.

Nice, considering it was the damned bicyclist who'd been riding on the sidewalk in the opposite direction from traffic.

Gritting his teeth, Nicky accelerated to head toward home. He might need a bandage over the scrape on his face, but he'd deal with that once he'd figured out things with his mom.

After sprinting the stairs, he hauled open the front door.

"Mom?" His shout met silence, nothing over the sound of the television. "Mom?" His mother was on the couch, asleep from what it looked like, except that her chest heaved on another cough.

She always looked pale in the reflection of the TV, but Nicky flicked on a light and saw that her lips were blue. "Shit!" He rushed to her side, feeling for her pulse and listening with an ear over her mouth for breathing. Both her heartbeat and her respiration were shallow.

Damn her for saying she didn't need an ambulance!

Nicky dialed 9-1-1 from the home phone next to the couch. His buddies at the station would most likely be the ones to come over. They'd get her to the hospital a hell of a lot faster than Nicky could get his mom's Lincoln out of the garage since the car hadn't been driven in months. Nicky cursed that he didn't have it in the driveway already, battery fully charged.

"This is 9-1-1, what is the nature of your emergency?"

Nicky gave all the information the dispatcher would need. Then he held his mom's hand and waited for her nine-hundred-dollar ride to the hospital to arrive.

Michael's phone buzzed from his messenger bag, and though it was against the law to use a cell while driving, he dug around to check the caller.

Nicky. Interesting that he'd finally called. Michael had given up on him since he hadn't heard from the guy in a week.

Checking his rearview, Michael pulled over. He answered the phone with a curt "Yeah?" because Nicky might have been hot as anything, but Michael didn't like to be kept waiting.

"Hi, Michael?" Nicky whispered as he spoke, his breathing as loud as his words. "It's, uh, Nicky. From the park."

"Yeah. I remember. Vaguely."

"Oh, yeah. Sorry." Nicky cleared his throat. "Actually, I haven't been able to get to the gym. So, um...I couldn't get that guy's number for you."

A likely story. Nicky looked like he'd never missed a day of working out in his life. "No worries." Michael checked his side-view mirror, making sure he'd have room to pull out once he got off the phone.

"I can go over this afternoon. See if he's around."

Michael had no idea why Nicky was dragging this out. He'd obviously just claimed to know a mechanic to get Michael's number, and then chickened out of calling. "Nah, that's okay. I'm happy enough with my regular guy."

"I think the shop is on Rainier," Nicky threw in.

"Well, that certainly narrows it down." Michael didn't care that he sounded bitchy.

"I mean, Rainier down by where I live. In Beacon Hill."

That still didn't give Michael much to go on. "Listen, thanks for trying, but—"

"I want to see you again." There was noise in the background like Nicky had gone outside and was standing by a busy road. "I...I wanted to call."

"If you had wanted to call me so badly, you would have." Michael quoted the combination of *He's Just Not That Into You* and Dr. Phil that he'd meditated on in the months following his breakup with Mark.

If a guy wants to call, he'll call. If he wants to be with you, he'll make it happen. How many times had he told as much to Henri in those first two years of college when Henri fell in lust with a different crush every week?

"I had some stuff come up in my personal life." Nicky's voice was low under the rumble of what sounded like a semi on his end.

Ah, yeah. The *lots of stuff going on* excuse. Michael had heard that line before. "Your thumb was busy? That's all you needed to dial a phone." Michael wasn't pissed Nicky hadn't called—it was the lie that annoyed him.

"No." Nicky didn't say anything for so long that Michael would have thought Nicky had hung up if it weren't for the road noises. "Hey, can you hold on just a sec? Give me a chance to get up to my room?"

Michael shouldn't be letting himself get roped in to whatever game Nicky was playing, but he settled back in his seat. "Fine."

"Cool." Nicky must have hit the mute button because all the sound on the line went dead.

A half minute later, Nicky's voice rasped, "You still there?"

"Yeah." The sun's angle glinted off one of the buildings, and Michael reached in the glove compartment to find his sunglasses. "I'm here."

"Cool." A breathy break in his whisper. "So, can we...uh...maybe meet in the same place?"

Behind the safety of his dark lenses, Michael rolled his eyes. "Seriously?" He had nothing against Volunteer Park, but the whole point of going somewhere like that was to have *anonymous* sex. Calling someone to arrange a meeting there seemed... Well, it seemed like they should have figured somewhere better this round.

"Yeah. I mean, if you want." Nicky sounded so hopeful it was hard to say no to him, though Michael knew he'd be better off keeping his distance.

"Whatever. Fine. You owe me a blowjob anyway."

Silence on the other end...but Michael waited, listening for Nicky's answer. Bottom line, Michael wasn't going to drag his heap of a car to Capitol Hill in the next couple days unless he'd be getting his dick sucked for the effort.

"Okay." Nothing in those two small syllables gave away what Nicky was thinking, but Michael's pulse still revved into high gear. He'd love a chance to see Nicky on his knees.

Brown eyes looking up at him, thick neck straining as Nicky struggled to get Michael into his throat... Michael couldn't be sure it would end up as sexy as his imaginings, but he was willing to give it a go. "So, tonight?"

"Sure. Yeah. And I'll try to get that number for you."

Michael chuckled. "Yeah, don't worry about it." He made his voice low and seductive, to hear if he could make Nicky's whisper rougher. "Just make sure to wear your leather jacket. You're going to need something for your knees."

"Where are you off to?" Nicky's mom tottered out of the kitchen holding a cup of tea. Her skin was still ashy pale, but according to her latest chest x-ray, the infection in her lower lungs had improved enough to let her come home. Nicky still felt she should be in the hospital on IV antibiotics. But unfortunately, he wasn't a doctor, and his mom's pulmonologist seemed to think pneumonia was a normal consequence once ovarian cancer spread to the liver and lungs.

Maybe he was right, but Nicky didn't have to like it.

Worse than her early release from the hospital, Nicky'd had to move a hospital bed into the living room for his mom to sleep on. With her breathing troubles, she got too winded climbing the stairs. Now every time he went into the living room, that bed mocked him, reminding him how his mother was far sicker than she'd been a few weeks ago.

"Do you want me to make you something to eat first?" His mother clasped her hands around her teacup, looking too frail to be standing, much less making anyone food.

"No, thanks." At least his mother's early release had qualified her for round-the-clock care from a home health aide. It would only last another week before Nicky had to pay a hefty co-pay to keep that level of care, but Nicky was grateful as hell to have help right now he didn't have to cover out of pocket.

"I'm going to a movie with a few of the guys from work." He kept busy checking the pockets of his jacket so he wouldn't have to look at her while he lied. Nicky's stomach twisted the same way it had as a kid. Fibbing had always given him a stomachache.

But he needed a break so badly he thought he'd jump out of his skin. Every waking hour in the past week he'd been at work or by his mother's side. Nicky didn't dare check the mirror before his date. He knew he looked like shit.

Good thing the park would be dark.

"Sounds like fun." As his mother passed, she squeezed then rubbed his arm. "Anything I would have heard of?"

"Probably not." The channels she watched ran commercials for medications and retirement plans, not trailers for the latest movies. Good thing too, since Nicky wouldn't have been able to name anything in the theaters. "Just some action film Cody wanted to see."

Darn it. Nicky babbled when he got nervous, and gave his mom too many details that he'd have to remember later.

"Well, I hope it's not too gruesome." Another squeeze and rub, this time heavier on the squeeze. Smiling up at him, she said, "My handsome boy," then continued her labored walk to the living room.

Michael's words batted around in his head—how Michael didn't go out with guys who wouldn't be seen with him in public. In other words, guys like Nicky. Not for the first time, Nicky wondered what his world would be like if he'd told his mother when he first had feelings about boys. He'd been so scared back then, and had wanted to tell someone.

But months had turned to years, and then she'd gotten sick...

He bent to kiss her forehead. "Have the nurse call me if you need me, okay?" He'd told the same to the health aide hanging out in the kitchen, watching shows on their other TV.

His mother waved him off. "Have fun, sweetheart."

Nicky hated driving his mother's car, but given how exhausted he was he didn't think it safe to take his bike. So he strolled down to where the Lincoln basked in the sunset like it had been reborn from its tomb in the garage. With a click of the key, the power locks opened, and Nicky slid into a front seat as spacious as a couch.

Billy Joel played on the radio, on one of his mother's CDs that was still in the player. Nicky had left it in the illusion that his mom might be able to take her car for a drive again. He didn't mind the music, though, so he sang along with the Piano Man as he pulled onto the street.

The couple times he'd driven since he brought his mom home from the hospital hadn't quite removed the stale-garage smell, so he pressed the power buttons to roll down the windows, and let the night air blow past.

Maybe Michael didn't date guys like him, but Nicky wouldn't be in his situation forever. He would never hope that anything bad would happen to his mother, but the truth was the truth. Whether he wanted it or not, she was going to pass away.

And when that happened...well, Nicky wasn't going to run out and start waving a rainbow flag. Certainly not right away.

But slowly...eventually... Some future version of him might be braver than the guy he was now, a version he caught a glimpse of when he thought about Michael.

The sky in the west shone pink along the horizon when he pulled into the parking lot. To his surprise, Michael already sat on the ledge alongside the steps that led down to the reservoir.

Nicky would have preferred to get out of the car without Michael seeing what he'd been driving, but unfortunately, Michael turned to look behind him.

His eyes widened in confusion—because, yeah, there weren't too many cars of Nicky's make and model driving around in the city—but then his gaze landed on Nicky, and Michael's shoulders shook in a laugh.

"Screw you," Nicky shouted to him, because he might be climbing out of a Town Car like an old man, but he wasn't going to let Michael snicker. "At least my car doesn't need a paint job."

Michael narrowed his eyes like he was trying to frown but ruined the effect by quirking his mouth back into a grin. "Hey, I'd rather be driving a..." Hopping off the ledge, he noticed the stitches on Nicky's cheek, and his mouth fell open.

Nervously, Nicky touched his face. There must have been a keychain attached to the side of that bicyclist's messenger bag. By the time the ambulance had arrived for his mom, Nicky's shirt had been red with blood.

"What the hell happened?" Michael walked toward him, all worried determination and forehead crumpled in concern.

"Got hurt on the bike." Nicky didn't want to get into a long explanation, especially not one that involved his mother. If he mentioned her, Michael might make any number of ridiculous, uninformed, inconsiderate comments. In five years of dealing with his mother's cancer, Nicky had heard them all—from how the disease could be cured by diet, or acupuncture, or bright lights, to how the medical establishment had some big cover-up and didn't even want to heal people.

After the week Nicky had, he couldn't handle hearing that type of bullshit from Michael, no matter how well-meaning.

"Was another driver at fault? Or the bike manufacturer? You're still getting paid while you're unable to work right? Because if the accident is—"

"Nah. It was just a few stitches. Nothing serious." Nicky could hear the exasperation in his own voice, but he wanted Michael to let it go. He needed to be swept away, gotten off. Kissed and touched. To be on break for a few hours.

Michael reached for his hand and wove their fingers together. "Okay. If that's all it was." He eyed Nicky's face, like he was trying to figure something out. "So you really did have stuff going on?"

Taken aback, Nicky smiled. "Yeah. Why? You didn't believe me?" With the tall tale he'd spun for his mom, Michael seemed like the only person Nicky actually told the truth to.

"I thought you hadn't wanted to call me." Despite his reddish hair, Michael wasn't as pale as Nicky. But Nicky could still make out a trace of blush on Michael's cheeks.

"I wanted to call." Before he could think, Nicky tilted his head, leaned in and pressed his mouth to Michael's. Their lips brushed together, messy and fast and a little off balance.

"Huh." Michael stepped closer, taking Nicky's kiss and upping the ante. "So, not only didn't you get me that guy's number, but you also didn't call when you wanted?"

Thoughts scrambled in Nicky's mind, fighting for primacy, but most of the ideas Nicky could string together were about getting his pants open and rubbing against Michael until both of them came. "I got you..." He dug in his pocket for the piece of paper with Harding Motors' number on it. Handing it over, Nicky felt his cheeks and neck getting hot. "I went by the gym and asked around, and the guy who runs the front desk told me the name of the shop." When he could finally stop his mouth from running, Nicky blinked into eyes that looked all the bluer against the purple sky. "And you said I owed you a..." God, he couldn't say it out loud, but he wanted it more than anything.

The slow spread of Michael's lips was the sexiest thing Nicky had ever seen. Better than porn, because in videos Nicky had always focused on the physical—an ass or a cock, thick thighs or the twirl of hair around a nipple.

He'd never searched a man's face before, noticed how the hard edges fought with soft lips and eyes.

"Yeah, you do." Michael reached for Nicky's belt loop. "But, no offense, you shouldn't be kneeling in the woods if you're injured." His tone was the same teasing drawl he often used. Maybe it was the set of his jaw, but Nicky was pretty sure Michael was honestly worried. "You could get dirt in it."

"Um..." There had to be a law against sex in parked cars, and Volunteer Park was crowded enough that any number of people could see them if they made out in the backseat. Somewhere else, maybe out at Sand Point, there'd be more privacy. "We could drive somewhere. Depending on what car you wanted to take."

"I rode over." Michael jutted his chin at a ten-speed locked on a nearby bike rack. "Well, part of the way, but then a bus came so I put the bike on the front rack." He paused, like maybe he was having the same problem Nicky was with babbling.

"We could take mine." Nicky opened his car door. Looking over his shoulder, he asked, "I mean, if you wanted."

Michael hesitated a second, but then bit his lip and held Nicky's door open for him. "Yeah, sure. Why not?" When Nicky slid into his seat, Michael closed his door and went around to his own side, in a backwards imitation of a guy taking a girl on a date. It felt right—like how they were supposed to be interacting, and Nicky was hit with the notion that maybe

Michael expected their relationship to follow that general boy/girl pattern. Nicky may not have talked to too many gay men, but he knew from poking around online that they often considered themselves tops or bottoms.

He'd never much thought about what category he fell into, since Nicky had been hoping to avoid ever having sex with a man, but now that he considered it, how he thought about sex sort of depended on what kind of guy he was imagining it with. With Michael, he didn't know what to expect. On the one hand, Michael was taller, but Nicky must have outweighed him by thirty pounds.

Nicky watched the way Michael sat—knees wide and elbow taking up a good half of the oversized armrest—and interpreted every move like an unconscious signal.

"Are we going?" Michael flashed him a smile.

"Oh. Yeah." There was no easy or straightforward way to ask Michael if he was a top in bed, so Nicky forced the thought to the back of his mind where it wouldn't cause any problems. They'd already agreed on what they were doing that night, so unless Michael planned on a round two—and with his bicycle stuck at Volunteer Park, they wouldn't have the time—fucking was off the menu.

Nicky twisted his key in the ignition, and the radio burst to life, blasting another of Billy Joel's greatest hits.

He rushed to change it to a radio station, but a couple guys near the edge of the water had turned to look their direction.

Teeth pressed tight together, Nicky forced himself not to duck. He didn't know these guys, would never see them again. And Michael had seemed so disgusted the last time Nicky had flinched around strangers.

"Sorry about that. This is my mom's car." Nicky reached to eject the CD.

"No worries." Michael smirked but didn't say anything as Nicky pulled out of the lot and headed over Capitol Hill.

Chapter Five

"Are you sure you're okay to be driving?" Michael hung on the handhold, feigning calm when Nicky once again rode up on the curb. The Town Car was built for wide suburban highways, not the crisscross of tiny streets in the city. It definitely wasn't built for the cramped traffic circles that had Michael certain Nicky would clip someone's mirror the next time he took a left. "Maybe you want to get on John. That's a straight shot if you're heading to MLK."

"I'm aiming for 23rd Street." Nicky kept his eyes on the road, his careful determination both sexy and sweet.

"Okay, but I'm not sure you can take a left from this street." Michael's fingers twitched, and when they came to another tight roundabout, he kicked at the spot where the brake would be.

"Oh shit, really?" Nicky rubbed the back of his neck. "Crap, I'll head to Seward Park, then, instead of Magnuson."

The skin between Nicky's collar and hair was a shade darker than the rest of him, like he'd somehow gotten sunburnt just there. Michael was drawn to that strip of skin. He wanted to taste to see if it was still warm. "Seward is a better call anyway. You never know if the University Bridge will be up."

"God, you're right." Nicky shook his head, the move making his curls dance around his ear.

The hair there looked soft, like Michael could twist it around his fingers while he kissed his way down Nicky's shoulder.

"So, what station do you want to listen to?" Nicky fiddled with the dial, clicking from one mass-produced song to the next.

"I liked what you had on before." Michael wasn't a fan of pop. Other than the occasional world music album that caught his attention, he normally listened to stuff from before the train wreck that was the 1990s.

"Really?" Nicky looked across the spacious front seat.

"Why not? It matches the vibe of the car."

"True." Nicky pulled into the long, empty driveway of Seward Park. The green space stretched around the south end of Lake Washington—many times the size Volunteer Park had been—and the parking area was only dotted with a few cars.

"So..." Nicky stopped the engine. "You want to, um...?" Nicky tugged at the front of his jean shorts, his gaze zeroed in on Michael's lap.

Some rebellious part of Michael's mind told him it wasn't fair to accept sexual favors from a guy who'd been in a motorcycle accident, no matter how mild, but that part sounded an awful lot like his mother. Having Nicky at his disposal made blood rush to Michael's dick, made his hiking shorts tighten around his hips.

"Yeah." Michael rubbed a hand over his bulge, struggling not to close his eyes and miss Nicky's nostrils flare with excitement. "You wanna move to the backseat?"

"Oh, um..." Nicky twisted to look behind them. "I guess."

They clamored out of the front and into the spacious backseat where Michael pulled Nicky into a kiss. He tasted like toothpaste and stubble and sunny days filled with oldies stations. His lips moved softly, as if he'd memorized the way Michael kissed and was falling back into the pattern.

When he pulled away, Nicky was breathless. "Okay." He landed a hand on Michael's lap, and his fingers probed to find the zipper. He bit his bottom lip, pink disappearing behind a crooked tooth, and if they weren't in a car, Michael would have ripped off every last shred of Nicky's clothes.

Lifting his hips, Michael helped the process. Luckily, Nicky covered Michael with a strong hand right away so Michael didn't have to suffer the indignity of being the only guy with his cock out in the backseat of a car.

"You should jerk off while you do it." Michael rubbed Nicky's back, urging his face down. He had no idea whether Nicky could manage while leaning across the seat, but Michael wanted to see Nicky's hand flashing, feel how close Nicky was to orgasm in the tightness of his lips.

"Okay." Nicky kissed a path over Michael's T-shirt. He lifted it at the bottom so he could kiss Michael's belly. When Nicky took the tip in his mouth, his lips were warm and wet. He felt his way around, tongue sliding.

Michael should have demanded Nicky give him more, but curiosity got the better of him. "So, what do you think?" He had no way to know if this was Nicky's first time giving a blowjob, but he would have bet a semester's tuition that Nicky hadn't done this before.

The only answer he got was Nicky whimpering as he moved lower, getting the top half into his mouth. This time, Michael couldn't resist the urge to tangle his hands through Nicky's hair. "You don't mind if I do this, right?"

Not everyone liked their head touched when they sucked a guy off.

Nicky looked up, eyes wide and pink lips damp. "Nah." His expression was lost, maybe even frightened. "I kind of like it."

Nothing Michael could do could stop him from grabbing Nicky's jaw right then, pulling him up and kissing that worry off his lips. Michael's heart thundered as he worked his tongue slowly inside.

Michael would pay for it tomorrow, and maybe the day after that, if he let himself get drawn in to Nicky emotionally. But for that night at least, Michael wanted to flick that switch, give in to that urge to kiss Nicky and hold him, maybe even mumble some crap he'd regret in the morning.

He didn't have any illusions—this was nothing more than a casual hook-up—but in that moment Nicky felt so perfect Michael decided to pretend.

"Oh God." Nicky pulled off, gasping. His gaze scanned everywhere. Over Michael's body, to the dick sticking out of Michael's pants, studying the features of Michael's face like he'd memorize the lines.

Michael did it right back. He shoved his hands up under Nicky's shirt, for the first time giving in to the temptation of those muscles. Palming the thick pecs, he gave both nipples a pass with his thumbs.

The skin under his fingers was taut, soft over muscle that felt like a solid, impenetrable wall. Ridges led across in all directions, cracks in armor.

When he reached for Nicky's fly, Nicky pushed his hands away. "No." Nicky bent to get back on Michael's cock. When his face was low enough for Michael to feel his breath, Nicky whispered, "I want to do it."

Then his mouth closed over Michael, fast and deep. Not to the bottom, but close enough that Michael couldn't help but grip handfuls of Nicky's hair to make sure Nicky didn't steal away that pressure.

Michael leaned back in his seat, body arching on reflex. Nicky's fingers worked into Michael's pants, cupping and cradling his sac, and though Nicky's desperate bobs wouldn't win any awards for finesse, they were enthusiastic enough to have Michael throbbing.

"You don't have to swallow." Michael's thighs tensed. He held back, not wanting to end it too quickly but knowing that he couldn't fight long.

With a desperate whimper, Nicky manipulated a hand between his legs, and though there was no way he could manage to jerk off in the position he was in, Michael could tell by his fitful twisting that Nicky was close too.

"Yeah... Fuck..." Then there was nothing but tight wetness and a sweet sense of connection as Michael rode to the crest of his orgasm.

The swell of it threw him back against the seat, legs shaking and discs of light spinning in his vision. He heard Nicky's moans, felt him struggling to keep sucking even though Michael could feel come dripping down his cock.

Nicky laid his face on Michael's thigh. Michael's hand was still in Nicky's hair, and Michael massaged, saying *thank you* with his fingertips since he wouldn't have known how to with words.

"Damn." Nicky lifted off, wiping his face. Between his frown and the quick swipes of his hand, he seemed upset.

Angry? Michael didn't think so. Or if Nicky was angry, it was only at himself.

"Need a wet wipe?" Maybe Michael should ask if Nicky was okay with what they'd done, but he couldn't imagine how to broach the subject. Worse, Michael suspected he wouldn't like the answer.

"Sure." Nicky accepted the packet Michael held out, pulling out an ammonia-scented towelette. Once he'd cleaned his face, he leaned back in his seat to check out the damage to the front of his pants.

"It's not obvious," Michael said by way of reassurance. A wet stain was spreading on the front of Nicky's underwear, but he hadn't gotten anything on his shorts.

"Yeah, right." There was a rueful pain in Nicky's eyes that got under Michael's skin and made his chest hurt.

"No, seriously. If you can get your underwear off..." Michael grabbed a tissue out of a box tucked behind the seat, and pulled at Nicky's waistband to clean his soft penis. "We'll dry you off." There was nothing Michael could do about what he suspected was Nicky's crisis of sexual identity, but at least Michael could help his physical predicament.

"There." He swiped a wet wipe around Nicky's base, making sure to avoid rubbing the chemicals on any part that would be too sensitive. The head was pink and tender, and Michael leaned down and gave it a kiss. Under his lips, the skin felt silky, fragrant with a mix of masculine heat and the kind of hardcore antibacterial cleaners Michael's own mom had never used but he'd envied at other peoples' houses.

"You don't have to do that." Nicky's hands fisted at his sides.

"I know I don't." Michael hid his expression by turning to stow the bits of paper by his feet. "That's why I want to."

Nicky turned pensive, like he was thinking too many things at once.

"So, you want to take those off?"

"Nah, I'm fine." Nicky closed up his jean shorts by their button fly then opened the door to head to the front.

As Michael followed, he braced for the brush-off. And fuck—he'd been expecting it, but it still made his throat tighten. "So, we going?" Michael dropped to the passenger seat, slamming the door a little harder than necessary. Eyes straight ahead, Michael gritted his teeth, waiting for Nicky to start the engine.

"I'm sorry I'm freaking out." Nicky's chuckle didn't cover the shakiness of his voice. "It's just...I hadn't done that before."

"Yeah. I figured." Michael splayed his legs so Nicky would know Michael didn't give a shit.

"Why? Was I bad?" Nicky's worry may have been cute—even funny—if Nicky hadn't been acting like Michael could go fuck himself.

Michael should have told Nicky he'd been terrible, given him a blow to his ego, but Michael sucked at lying. "No. It was fine. You just seemed nervous."

"Oh. Well, yeah." Nicky gazed past Michael and out the window at the lake. "I guess I was." His move tentative, Nicky reached for Michael's hand. "I..."

"You don't want to hook up again." Michael figured he'd put the guy out of his misery. "It's cool. I get it." He'd already told Nicky he didn't date guys in the closet.

"No, I mean...I want to do this again." Nicky tugged at Michael's hand like he wanted Michael to look at him. In the dark it was impossible to tell where his pupils ended and the irises began. And Nicky's puffy lower lids made him always look like he'd been crying. Either that, or like he was just waking up. "You liked it, right?"

Michael didn't know how to answer, so he ground his teeth, weighing the potential pain against the definite pleasure. There were plenty of things he still wanted to do with Nicky, to him even, if Nicky was game. But there were reasons Michael didn't get involved with guys like Nicky—and it wasn't all because Michael didn't want to get hurt. Nicky would never grow or learn to deal with his same-sex feelings if Michael pretended that staying closeted was a viable long-term choice.

"I did like it." Michael took his hand back, gently so Nicky wouldn't take it as a rejection. "But maybe if you want to be doing this kind of thing regularly, you might want to see a counselor or something. Figure out where you stand."

Michael had worked a hotline the first couple years of undergrad where he'd taken calls from kids questioning their sexuality. Talking academically about whether or not you were gay was always easier than the nitty-gritty of actual relationships. "Are you bi?"

Nicky backed up until the better part of his body was against the door. "What do you mean?"

Michael rolled his eyes. "Okay, yeah. Clearly you have some work to do figuring this out."

A police car rolled through the park, and Michael checked the time on the car's digital display. "Looks like they're going to be closing the gates."

"Yeah." With a sigh that said he hadn't gotten the response from Michael that he wanted, Nicky started the car. "We should probably go." He pulled onto the road that led along the lake.

Lights flickered in houses and buildings on the other side, and sparse blue clouds floated across the navy sky. A couple stars were out—or they may have been airplanes.

Michael hadn't done something like this in as long as he could remember, gone for a night drive with a guy he'd been intimate with. Junior year he'd dated that floppy skinny guy for a while, but that hadn't lasted beyond spring break. Joseph had been a little too fem for Michael's tastes, even though he'd been everything Michael wanted in bed.

Too bad Nicky was so clearly confused. Michael might have liked someone to hang out with for more time than it took to suck each other off.

"So...you'd be up for doing this again if..." Nicky pushed like he wanted an ultimatum, some agreement that would make him *gay enough* or *out enough* to meet Michael's standards.

But it wasn't as simple as being seen in public together, or as black-and-white as coming out at work. It came down to whether a guy was comfortable in his own skin. Not vacillating all the time, or jacking Michael with his hand while hating Michael in his heart.

No step-by-step guidelines would get Nicky to that place, though Michael wished Nicky were there already.

"Why don't you think about it?" Michael watched the lake go by, the window cracked open and letting in the sweet summer smells. A comforting sadness twisted in his belly. "Call me when you figure it out."

In Michael's heart of hearts, he knew Nicky would call whether he'd decided anything about himself or not. Maybe it was Michael who needed a few days to cool off and get some perspective.

"Okay." Nicky's voice was quiet and perfectly serious when he muttered, "I will."

Chapter Six

By the time Nicky pulled into the driveway and maneuvered the Lincoln between the abandoned planters and the trash cans he had to remember to take down to the curb the next day, his underwear had fully adhered to his dick.

The awkwardness of getting out of the car with his jean shorts shrink-wrapped around his hips was nothing, though, compared to the thoughts battering inside his skull.

Are you bi?

Nicky had never considered the question. He'd spent so many years trying not to be the other thing that he hadn't stopped to consider the intermediate option. Early in high school, he'd stared in the mirror, thinking *I'm not gay* over and over, never daring to say it out loud but hoping repeating the words in his head could make them true.

The lights flickering behind the window shades showed that his mom was still awake, so there'd be no way of avoiding her. Would she see guilt in him? Funny, but Nicky had seldom felt guilty before when he'd gone to the park.

Sure, the first time there'd been guilt, but not any more than the first time he hid a porno under his bed or masturbated into a sock. It was all the same shame, the same cold spot in his stomach.

This was different. Not shame—not the feeling that he was fighting a desire bigger than himself and that lust was winning. This guilt was purer, and lust had very little to do with it.

His steps set the rotten planks of the front steps creaking, and Nicky thought about the wood he'd need and when he'd find time to replace them. He thought of anything but the way he'd felt at Seward Park, with Michael kissing him and happier than he'd ever been in his life.

"Is that you, Nicky?" his mom called.

"Yeah." He wished he could say good night quickly, then run upstairs and avoid her like he had a few times in high school, but he no longer had the luxury of that kind of disrespect. Nicky grabbed a sweatshirt off the bench by the door and held it in front of him as he went into the living room.

"Did you have a nice time?" Her forehead was creased and her eyes tense. Nicky suspected it was because of her pain, but he couldn't ignore the needle of worry that she was angry with him.

"Yeah. The movie was great." Nicky tried to ignore the hospital bed, though it kept drawing his gaze.

She coughed gently and leaned forward from her spot on the couch to get her cup of water. Her skin seemed so thin now. Much thinner than a week ago, and had a tinge of yellow under the surface. "You weren't gone long enough for a movie." Her voice was soft, and he could tell by how she swallowed that she was trying hard not to cough.

It took Nicky the space of three breaths to realize she was teasing him. Now that he looked, he could see that she was trying to smile.

"Yeah. We didn't end up going. Just had a beer instead." Nicky couldn't tell what hurt worse, seeing her in pain or the guilt clawing his way up his throat and threatening to choke him. Stepping across the coffee table, he settled next to her on the couch.

He put his arm around her and eased her into a hug. She felt so brittle, like one wrong word and she'd break. When he was a kid, she'd been so strong. Only five foot three, but a whirlwind of energy.

He missed that part of her so much, the strength he could turn to whenever he needed more than his own, her arms gripping him tight even when he'd grown a half-foot taller than her.

"Is something wrong, Nicky?"

He pulled away, getting himself back together. She needed him to be tough, not searching for the parent who was no longer there. "No." He wiped his face. His nose was running a little, but his eyes had managed to stay dry. "I'm fine."

"Is it about that girl? You know if you're seeing her, you can tell me."

"It's not about a girl." At least for once he was telling his mother the truth.

"Why do we have to stop at your mom's place again?" Henri cranked the handle, trying to lower the window on Michael's car.

"She wants me to pick up some tomatoes." Michael leaned across the seat and slapped Henri's hand. "Stop it. You'll break the thing." Michael hated how his mother thought he would come running every time she called. In fact, visiting his mom was almost ruining his buzz of contentment over his night with Nicky.

He was walking a slippery slope, risking getting emotionally involved, but damn he hadn't felt so good with a guy in ages.

"Geez. When in the hell are you going to trade this thing in for something that doesn't stink like an oil spill?"

"It's not so bad." Michael rolled down his window to get some cross ventilation. Much as he hated to admit it, his car was starting to reek. The last three bouts of repairs had gotten her running again, but hadn't done much for the stench of gasoline every time he turned over the engine. "And anyway, I can't afford a new one."

The light flicked to green, and the cars rolled forward. Unfortunately, the light ahead of that one turned red, so the traffic stuttered to a halt before Michael even got through the first.

"With the money you put in to fixing this heap..." Henri trailed off, probably because they'd bickered like an old married couple over Michael's car a hundred times.

"God, I hate driving to Wallingford." As an undergrad, Michael had liked having his mom nearby for holidays. It saved time since he had to drive all the way out to Snoqualmie for Christmas to see his father and *the bitch* he'd left Michael's mom for. But now that he was older, he wished his mom lived farther away.

"Well, why didn't you tell her no?"

Michael rolled his eyes. Henri's question must have been rhetorical because both of them knew the answer. His mom would call and hound him, and eventually show up at his apartment huffing and whining that she couldn't reach him.

A familiar tension curled under Michael's skin as he turned onto his mother's street.

"Oh, man." Henri pointed at the front of Michael's mother's house.

She hadn't been lying about needing someone to take her tomatoes. Seven buckets of plants lined the wall in front, all heavy with bright red fruit.

Giant sunflowers arched into her neighbor's yard. Purple, yellow and red-streaked edible greens exploded in bouquets out of the planting box in front of her dilapidated fence.

As Michael slowed to park, she bounded out her front door, garden gloves over arms bare to the shoulders. Her wild, gray hair flew around the edges of her haphazard bun.

"Hey, Mom." Michael shoved his door shut with his hip a few times. "The garden looks good."

"Uh-huh. I told you I didn't want to see you driving that anymore." She tossed her gloves to the side and folded her arms across her bosom.

If he hadn't been gay already, his mom's chest would have made him so. The woman never wore a bra. Not ever. Michael understood her point that underwires were the modern equivalent of a corset and bra straps a tool of the oppressor, but he'd always wished she'd tie down the girls when he had friends over.

"I can't afford a new car, Mom."

"Oh, please!" She shuffled down the path to plant a kiss on his cheek and one on Henri's. "I know it has sentimental value. But...well, don't you think you're done punishing yourself?"

Henri faked a sudden interest in the hydrangeas cascading down the southeast wall of the two-bedroom cottage. Despite his impeccable acting abilities, he couldn't seem to find an excuse to get all the way to the backyard, so Michael hissed as he tried to head off his mom's argument. "The fact that my ex gave me the car has nothing to do with it."

He and Mark had broken up four years ago. The car hadn't belonged to Mark in ages. "It's the only car I have, and it would be worthless as a trade-in."

His mother cocked an eyebrow at the purple Mustang. "Some of these new hatchbacks get forty miles to the gallon on the highway. You wouldn't even need to get a hybrid."

"Mom, I'm not getting—"

"When I trade in the Subaru, I'm going to get one of those new Smart Cars. You could—"

Michael's throat clogged with annoyance, so he raised his voice. "I don't *want* a new car!"

The car didn't remind him of Mark, but it did remind Michael of how he'd felt back when they'd first started dating— sixteen and escaping his mom's house to go to seedy bars and even seedier hotels. His ex had been a closeted asshole, but his car had given Michael freedom.

"I'm only saying I think it might be healthy for you to move on." She waddled over to her gardening bench and pulled open the lid to dig around inside. Maybe he was being unkind thinking of it as waddling, but there was a lot more lateral movement in her steps than there had been a few years earlier.

She pulled a couple reusable shopping bags out of the bench, as well as a folding basket with watermarks up the sides. "You could have a ceremony..." She handed him the containers and walked, hips swaying under her sundress, toward the door.

He hoped she was wearing underwear. "A ceremony for what?"

Her house was just like he remembered. Wallpaper clashed with hanging art, and statues, plants and pictures cluttered every available surface. When his dad had first left, the house had been clean most of the time. Michael still remembered how he and his mom had sat in the living room that first night after his dad was gone, cross-legged and eating gluten-free, soy-cheese pizza. His mom had lit candles and called them *refugees of love.*

At the time, it had sounded like poetry.

"For the *'stang*, of course!" His mother always called his car that when she wanted to annoy him.

"A funeral for my car?" He dropped his bags on the kitchen island in the narrow space between a crate of summer squash and a stack of unopened mail.

His mother ran the faucet into a sink full of beets—their long leaves sticking over the edge to drip pink water on the floor. How his mother managed to keep the work for the courses she taught clean in the midst of all this dirt was beyond him.

"Not a funeral…" She scrubbed the beets with a brush. "More like a clearing of spirits."

"So, an exorcism?" It wouldn't be the first time his mother tried to force Michael to get rid of something she didn't like by smothering it in burning sage. Back in high school, she'd tried to murder Michael's favorite pair of ripped jeans on a funeral pyre.

"There's no need to be melodramatic." His mother shook out the beets, spraying Michael's white shirt with red, and shoved them in the bag. "I just mean it might be easier if you had some closure with…you know who."

"We broke up four years ago, Mom." The last word came out on a groan worthy of a fifteen-year-old.

"But you still have his car."

Michael straightened abruptly. "Where are the tomatoes?"

His mom pursed her lips but in the end must have decided to stop pestering him, because she went to the cupboard to pull out another bushel of vegetables. Shiny Romas dotted a layer of green-and-brown heirlooms.

"Well, are you seeing someone else yet? I thought you and Henri…" She laid a few sheets of old newspaper in the bottom of the basket, articles on marijuana legalization dancing in big green letters alongside op-eds.

"No." His knee-jerk reaction was to mention Nicky, but he kept his mouth shut. After all, three hook-ups didn't count as dating. And even if it did, his mother would give him all kinds of crap about it. "Henri is seeing someone new, and to be honest I really don't have time for a relationship now."

His mom narrowed her eyes. "You're not seeing someone in secret again, are you? You know, it's not a real relationship if you can't be open that you're together."

Her question bore right into the center of him and set a fuse on his temper. "No. I'm not seeing anyone in any capacity." Grabbing the other two bags of food off the overcrowded counter, he backed to the door. Damn her for going straight for the kill. Maybe he wouldn't have snuck around so much if his mom hadn't been against Mark from the beginning.

A tiny part of him, some corner of his chest he didn't unlock except in his most pathetic bouts of melancholy, wondered if things with Mark would have been different if they'd been able to hang out at Michael's house as a couple.

Maybe if Mark had seen not everyone would judge him for being gay…

No. Michael had to get that out of his mind before he went into the kind of tailspin that had him on antidepressants the better part of his sophomore year.

"I need to go." Michael had a few things to do that afternoon, and desperately wanted a jog to clear his mind.

"Well, come around next week. The pole beans are just about ready to harvest."

Michael made it to the door where Henri was lazily picking flowers off a twig of thyme.

"You ready?" Henri tossed the bare stem into a bush.

"Yeah." Michael couldn't bring himself to wave to his mom as he left, so he let Henri say goodbye for the both of them. He was being a brat, considering she'd just given him food, but he couldn't get over her little barb about him sneaking around.

Anyway, going to parks wasn't sneaking. Neither was hanging around the third-floor bathroom in the sociology building. Certainly, seeing Nicky wasn't sneaking any more than picking up someone on Grindr. What the hell did his mother want, a phone call every time he was about to put his dick in some guy's mouth?

His trunk hadn't opened without a fight since his junior year, so Michael shoved the bags in the backseat and started the car.

"Smells a lot nicer in here now." Henri's smile was benign enough, but Michael could tell Henri was struggling not to smirk.

"Whatever. Do you want some squash to take home?"

Michael pulled away from the curb, hoping his car didn't sputter the way it usually did when it first got going. Of course his mom was watching from the yard, waving to them over the fence like he was leaving for college for the first time, not going back to his apartment two miles away.

"The only things I can imagine me and Logan doing with a squash are dirty." Henri crossed his legs primly.

Michael snorted. Thank goodness his friend had come along for the ride or Michael would have wanted to rip the steering wheel from its stem.

Nicky didn't have to go to work, so he slept in. Dreams of ginger hair and strong hands blended with the moments he was awake and thinking about Michael, until in the end he gave in to the fantasy and jerked off.

As he lay staring at his ceiling afterwards, he knew he had to come up with some kind of shift in his thinking. He could head to the gym later, burn off some of the stress in his muscles, but with another two days off before his next shift, Nicky would go nuts if he couldn't figure out what came next with his sex life.

He didn't want things to stop with Michael. If anything, he wanted things to move faster until the two of them... He didn't know what to picture. Nicky had never had a girlfriend, so he didn't know what people did when they were dating. TV made it seem like people went to restaurants and dance clubs and movies, but Nicky didn't know if gay guys did the same kinds of things.

After pushing out of bed, he made his way downstairs and to the bathroom. A man's voice, Father MacKenzie's, carried from the living room, along with the lighter tones of his mom.

Nicky hoped the good Father wasn't tipping up her coffee with anything. Day drinking with a friend was the right of any person who'd been through as much as his mother, but it couldn't have been nine a.m. This time in the morning, she was often still nauseous from her antibiotics and painkillers from the night before.

His own face stared back at him as Nicky brushed his teeth. He looked like his dad, or the way his dad had looked in the pictures his mom still had.

Nicolas Senior had seemed like a ghost in the house, coming and going on tours overseas. Until one day his mom got a phone call saying he'd died in a Jeep accident.

His father hadn't had Nicky's eyes, though. Not with the roundness and tilt that Nicky had always worried gave him away.

After spitting his toothpaste in the sink and washing the stubble off his razor, he thought about what to say to his clean-shaven self. His mom and Father MacKenzie were talking. They wouldn't hear. It would just be his ears, and God's. As far as Nicky could tell, if God had wanted to strike him down, he would have done so already.

"I'm..." He'd meant to say "bi", but the syllable hung on his lips. That was the kind of half-lie he might have been willing to settle for when he was younger, if he'd had the guts to walk this road when he was still in high school.

"I'm gay." The words felt foreign enough that he cocked his head at his reflection, wondering if the guy in the mirror was any different from the one who'd faced him the previous morning.

"Yeah." He scrubbed his jaw, chuckling. "I am."

Somehow before this, there'd always been a doubt in his mind, despite all the evidence. Maybe it had been Michael's dick in Nicky's mouth that did it, but Nicky didn't think so. The night before last, he'd felt powerful and desirable, like he was gaining this whole side of himself that had been locked away.

Next to the mirror hung a picture of fields stretched out and leading to a lake—a cheap knockoff of some famous painting Nicky didn't know the name of. He could see why his mom liked it enough to keep it somewhere they'd both see it every day. The painting was about hope.

"Nicky?" Father MacKenzie called down the hall.

"Yeah?"

"Your mother needs to talk to you about some things." That sounded ominous enough to set Nicky on edge and make him forget about the shower he'd been about to take.

He grabbed a shirt out of the hamper and pulled it over his head. "I'll be right there."

For once, the TV was off. Father MacKenzie sat in a hard-backed chair, his hands folded between his knees.

"Good morning, Nicky." Father MacKenzie stood. He'd known their family forever, married his parents and baptized Nicky. Though Nicky hadn't been to weekly mass since he was in high school, he still went to church for Christmas and Easter.

"G'morning, Father." Nicky ducked his head in respect.

Father MacKenzie held his hand a little longer than Nicky would have expected. His fingers were bony and cool, but the warmth in his face was undeniable. "How are you holding up?"

"Oh, fine." Nicky pulled his hand away. Those searching eyes saw way more than Nicky wanted. Sure, his buddies at the station knew about his mom's condition. The home healthcare aides and the nurses and doctors at the hospital knew as well. But Father MacKenzie was the only person he considered like a friend who saw Nicky's day-to-day life.

"Well, you're doing a great job around here." Father MacKenzie nodded at the house. Nicky guessed he meant that the place wasn't a complete disaster and Nicky and his mother weren't living in squalor.

Nicky had seen a couple of his friends' bachelor pads. Dirty dishes and old pizza boxes sat on their coffee tables, and their carpets hadn't been vacuumed in weeks. Nicky couldn't imagine his mom living somewhere like that. She'd exhaust herself trying to clean.

"Thanks." Nicky grabbed a chair from its spot against the wall and pulled it to the opposite side of the couch from where Father MacKenzie was sitting. "So what's up?" He forced his tone to be light and conversational, even though he could feel tension churning in the room.

"Your mother..." Father MacKenzie started, but his mom reached from her spot on the couch like she'd take his hand.

Father MacKenzie met her halfway so she didn't have to lean so far.

With her hand linked with the priest's, his mother turned to him. "Nicky, I think it's time we talked about my living somewhere else."

Something clicked in Nicky's chest, pumping adrenaline through him as hard as if the alarm had just gone off at the station. Trying to keep his voice even, he answered, "You want us to move?" Maybe she wanted them closer to the hospital. They could sell the place and move into an apartment, though Nicky wondered if the stress of seeing all her belongings packed in boxes might be too much for her.

"Nicky." Her eyes sparkled as she teased him. She must have taken a pain pill pretty recently, because her smile was more relaxed than he'd seen from her since she came back from the hospital. "You know what I'm talking about. It's time we started talking about residential care."

So fast he got a crick in his neck, Nicky twisted his gaze away. A statue sat on top of the television—Virgin Mary nested in a couple of doors that opened on hinges. Most of his mom's artwork was tasteful, but the background on this statue was gold and the folds of Mary's robe hung in bright shades of pink and blue that Nicky was fairly certain hadn't existed in the ancient textile industry. The baby in her arms had curly hair.

Nick wiped a hand across his eyes.

"You've been better, though." Nicky couldn't drag his attention away from his mom's menagerie on top of the TV set. When he was little, his grandma had visited and told him the name of every one of those saints. She'd passed when he was in high school, and Nicky wished so badly now that he'd paid attention enough to remember.

"We both know that's not true." When his mother scooted forward on the couch, Father MacKenzie rushed to help her. His mom closed her hand around his, squeezing, though her grip wasn't all that firm. "We've talked about this, Nicky. Back when I first got sick."

"What about Saundra? And Jessica, and Miguel. I'll have to pay part of it out of pocket, but we can keep their rotation." Even as he said it, Nicky knew he was being unreasonable. They'd been through all this before, crunched the numbers and looked at all the angles back when his mother's end-of-life plan had still seemed far away.

"You know that won't work with your schedule." His mother's voice was quiet but firm with the kind of strength Nicky had heard so many times in childhood. Any time he misbehaved or his mom needed a quiet moment to herself, all she'd had to do was use *that tone* and Nicky knew she meant business.

Nicky wanted to rail against her, shout at her to stay, beg her not to leave.

"I get it." He patted her hand, rubbing as hard as he dared on her crepe-paper skin. "It's okay. We can start looking at places."

Maybe once he showed his mother what her options were, she'd realize she didn't want to go. They'd figure out how to pay for an aide who could be at the house during Nicky's twenty-four-hour shifts. There had to be a way Nicky could get more time off work, or take another leave of absence.

"Actually, Father MacKenzie's recommended something." His mother smiled gently.

"Good." Nicky made his face as blank as possible. "That's great." He had to get out of there. Work out his anger in the pump of metal in his hands and the scream of his muscles.

"Wonderful." His mom relaxed onto the sofa. Her eyes drooped like the conversation had taken all her strength.

Nicky felt like shit for making her worry. Of course he'd support her decision. "I love you, Mom." Nicky bent over the couch to kiss her on the cheek.

Chapter Seven

Michael still hadn't heard back from Nicky's mechanic about what was wrong with his engine. Stupid as it was, he kept worrying that it boded poorly for his car, and that was why he took it upon himself to clean under the espresso machine and behind the cabinets at Speedy Coffee. His nose was stuffy from the dust, but once he'd taken all the displays apart and hauled everything away from the walls, he was able to get behind the cabinets with a spray bottle of Windex and a Swiffer.

His phone rang in his pocket, and Michael set his rag on the table to answer.

"Hello?"

"Hey. Um…it's me. Nicky."

"Oh. Yeah." Michael grinned. "Hi."

"Yeah." Nicky cleared his throat, his voice dropping deeper. "I was just wondering if maybe… I don't know if I could get away for as long as a movie. But maybe dinner?"

"I'm not sure there was an invitation in there." Michael used a paper clip to clean between keys on the cash register, cautious in his response. "And what do you mean you can't get away?"

"It's a long story."

"I bet." Michael had been looking forward to Nicky calling. More excited than he should have been. But he had to ask. "If you're seeing someone, I don't think—"

"I'm not dating anyone else." Nicky's voice picked up strength. "I've just got a lot going on."

Maybe it was the annoyance in Nicky's voice that set Michael off, but Michael had been through the ringer of *I've been busy* and *there's a lot going on in my life* enough that he wouldn't settle for excuses.

"So much going on that you can't go to a movie? Funny, you seem to have the time to get your dick sucked." Okay, that was a low blow, and probably something Michael had wanted to say to Mark so often that he was spewing it at Nicky for no reason.

But shit, Tomas was a firefighter and had plenty of time to date Jesse. And Logan didn't do anything beside work and hang on Henri's every word.

"My mom is sick."

Michael wasn't sure he'd heard right. Some part of him wanted to snap off a remark about how that was *a likely story*, but Michael held back. "Oh." Not knowing how close Nicky was with his mother, Michael wondered whether to ask for more information. He didn't have a right to all of Nicky's personal details, but it seemed rude not to say something. "Like...is she okay?"

"Yeah." Nicky let out a rueful chuckle. "Well, not really. Not by any normal standards."

Michael chewed on the inside of his cheek, his jaw working. Clearly, there was a story there, but Michael wasn't sure how much to probe. "So, do you need to hang out with her? Or take her to the doctor? I mean, we can do dinner some other time."

"No." Nicky sighed. "Her home health aide had an open slot and can come in tonight for a few hours, and I..." His voice wavered, almost cracking. "I really need to get out of here. Do something normal." Another laugh, but this one more amused than sad. "Well, not something normal. Maybe a little...less normal, actually."

Home health aide... That meant Nicky's mother was the kind of sick that went beyond a course of antibiotics, or even surgery and a week or two of recovery.

Michael wanted to ask a million questions—if Nicky's dad was in the picture, or any siblings. But he got from the tone of Nicky's voice that Nicky wanted to forget about all that for a while. "Less normal, huh?" Michael leaned against the counter. "What kind of *less normal* are we talking? A leather bar?"

Nicky's snort was pure mirth. "No. Okay, not that un-normal. I was thinking maybe Chinese?"

"I could do that." After a day of coffee shop food, Michael was more than ready for some vegetables. "You want to go to the International District?" There were some great Thai and Indian places in the U District, but all the best Chinese was in the I.D. "Shit." He remembered his car was still at the auto place down on Rainier. "My car's in the shop."

"Oh. Well, I could pick you up."

"I guess." Michael dreaded the thought of being a passenger again. "Or I could meet you. There's a bus that goes straight from The Ave to Madison."

"You don't have to do that. I don't mind coming up that way. What's the address?"

"It's on The Ave. The place is Speedy Coffee. Knock hard. I may be in the back office."

"Awesome." Michael could hear Nicky's smile over the phone. "And by the way, thanks."

"For what?"

"For agreeing to meet me. I know... Well, I've thought a lot about what you said." Nicky let the words hang there. "I mean, about my being not straight."

Henri had told Michael a thousand times that "I told you so" was Michael's personal catch phrase, but hearing Nicky admit Michael was right...out loud...well, it went a long way to puffing up Michael's pride.

"Yeah. Well, I'm starving, so hurry up." Michael chuckled, covering up his excitement.

"I should be there in twenty minutes."

Nicky would never find street parking. Especially not for the Lincoln, which seemed to have been built with the assumption that the owners would always be going somewhere with valet parking.

Luckily, Michael stood on the curb, in front of a café tucked between one of those lunchtime-only noodle places and a head shop. The sign in the window was lower than the rest on the street, giving it the aura of somewhere you'd only go if you were on foot.

Michael hurried to the car and hopped in. The few people lined up behind Nicky might not have been thrilled with him stopping, but at least none of them honked.

"Hey." Nicky tried to smile.

Michael was gorgeous in a shirt that was a muted, almost pastel color of green. "Thanks for picking me up." He tossed a messenger bag in the backseat. When he settled back, his smile was tentative but kind. "I could have taken the bus."

"Nah. I wanted the drive." After spending the day touring the hospice center with his mother, and then talking on the phone for hours with her doctor and their health insurance, the thrum of traffic was almost meditative.

Nicky realized he must have been staring into space when he caught a glimpse of Michael's expression. "Oh." He rubbed his face. "Sorry." He felt a rush of embarrassment.

"Are you okay?" Michael's eyes were searching, looking for something Nicky didn't want anyone to see. Michael was like Father MacKenzie, but worse. Because Father MacKenzie saw all the ways Nicky was strong, but Michael only ever seemed to see him when he was weak.

"Yeah." He rubbed the heel of his hand across his eyes. "It's just we're admitting her to a hospice center soon." He couldn't believe he was telling as much to Michael, but Nicky couldn't seem to stop the words from pouring out. "And in order for her to be admitted, her doctor had to certify she had only six months left..."

He'd known it wouldn't be much more than that. He'd prepared for it from day one. But to deal with pencil pushers over the phone debating the length of his mother's remaining life and what they'd be willing to dole out to make her comfortable was almost more than he could bear.

Before he knew it, tears were dripping down his face—more than he'd cried since he'd first heard about her diagnosis. Hell, worse maybe than he'd cried since he was a kid.

"Pull over." Michael gripped Nicky's leg.

"I..." Nicky's hands shook. Traffic streamed to his left and right, and the curb was packed with wall-to-wall cars. He couldn't have pulled off if he wanted to.

"There." Michael put a hand on Nicky's arm and pointed to a giant sign that said *Parking.* "Pull in there. Now. You can't be driving like this."

Without answering, Nicky did as directed. The parking lot was cramped, with no way to turn around, but at least Nicky was off the road and no longer a danger to himself or other drivers.

"You okay?" Michael grabbed Nicky's hand, rubbing his palm.

Sure, at the gym Nicky could have lifted more than Michael. But today, in life, Nicky wanted to collapse and let Michael take his weight. "Yeah." He leaned his head back in the seat, eyes hot but no longer leaking. His heart pattered with anxiety. "I'm okay."

"Well, get out. I'm driving."

In truth, Nicky had been expecting a hug. The way Michael slammed out his side of the door and came around to Nicky's side bordered on angry.

"Come on." Michael reached inside, helping Nicky out of his seat.

Nicky wanted to tell Michael he was perfectly fine to be driving, but still shaking from his meltdown, Nicky didn't argue. "Sorry. I—"

Michael crushed their mouths together in a fast kiss. "Listen. I know you're upset." He squeezed Nicky's hand right there in the parking lot in Eastlake. The sun hadn't set, but Nicky couldn't be bothered to care anymore. It was hard to care about anything when he'd hadn't slept in days and he needed to buy boxes to pack his mother's stuff.

"Let's get somewhere we can talk." Michael glanced around the parking lot. They were next to a restaurant, but it was

Italian, not Chinese, and looked expensive. "Or we can eat here. Assuming we can coax this monster into a parking space."

Nicky's laugh was watery, but he liked the feeling of Michael's fingers laced with his. "Here's fine. I guess." Nicky bit his lips, staring at their joined hands.

"Is this okay?"

"Yeah." Nicky tried to sound casual. "Yeah, it's fine."

Michael pulled him in for a hug—kind of like a bro hug, but different in the way Michael caressed his back.

Then Michael took the keys from Nicky's hand and got in the front seat of the Town Car. In a few seconds, and with a feat of driving prowess Nicky never would have expected, Michael maneuvered into a spot.

He had to work to squeeze out the door, but the car was safely inside the painted white lines.

"How'd I do?" The strut in Michael's step went a long way to helping Nicky's mood.

"Good." Nicky doubted he'd be able to pull off suave, but he made his best effort. "Better than I would have thought."

Grinning, Michael shoved him in the arm. Again, more intimate than straight guys touching, but it still felt perfectly normal. "I've heard this restaurant is pretty good." Michael pushed the door open but waited for Nicky to go through. Nicky couldn't help feeling like it was another one of those male/female gestures, and Michael was signaling things about their relationship.

"You like Italian, right?" Michael asked close to his ear.

"Yeah. A lot." Nicky wondered if he was whispering. He certainly felt out of breath.

"Cool." Michael touched the low part of Nicky's back. The restaurant was dark and crowded enough that Nicky was pretty sure no one noticed.

A young and very blonde hostess led them to their table. When she gave them their menus, she flashed Michael a smile, then one at Nicky, like she knew perfectly well they were together.

Some kind of opera played in the background, and candles lit the tables. With their booth enclosed from the others it felt like a real date, and to Nicky's surprise, nothing about it seemed weird.

"So. Are you a pasta man? Or do you go more for sausage?" Michael twitched his lips to the side.

Nicky checked out the platters of spaghetti being placed in front of a man and woman at a table across from them. "I bet a plate that size is a week's worth of carbs." A second too late, Nicky realized he probably sounded like a freak with an eating disorder. He cleared his throat. "I mean, not like I care about that stuff."

Under the table, Michael touched his thigh. "Well, I didn't assume you looked so good on accident."

Nicky couldn't help but chuckle right along with Michael. His friends at the station always ate whatever they wanted. Sure, they worked out, but not the way Nicky did. Not because they got off on looking in the mirror when their muscles were ripped. "Well, yeah. The guys at the gym can be a little hardcore."

Plenty of his workout buddies were way more religious than Nicky about what they ate. Nicky glanced at the menu and tried really hard not to calculate the fat and protein content of each option.

"Well, I grew up gluten-free, so a place like this is like a candy store."

"Wow. Seriously?"

"Yup." Michael's leg brushed Nicky's under the table. "I lived for eating pizza at friends' houses."

When the waitress came, Michael ordered a half-carafe of wine, and although Nicky usually drank beer, he went along with the vibe of Michael taking charge. They both gave their orders, and her smile as she left them took away the last of Nicky's worry that she might judge them for being together.

Nicky couldn't stop thinking about that warm hand on his back as he walked in the door. He wished there were some subtle way of asking about Michael's preference in bed without being awkward.

"So. Are you from here? Or a transplant?" Michael's foot knocked against Nicky's again, making Nicky wish the tablecloth was longer and Michael could rub their legs together while they talked.

"My parents moved here from Rhode Island, but I was born here." The booth was U-shaped, and Nicky scooted toward the deeper part of the U so they could speak more quietly. "How about you? Did you move here for school?"

"Nope. Larson is as Scandinavian-Northwesterner as it gets. My dad works in financials for Weyerhaeuser and my mom teaches—they're divorced—but my grandfather and his father worked for logging companies out in Aberdeen."

Well, the Nordic thing certainly explained Michael's complexion, as well as his height. "O'Brian." Nicky smiled. "Whole family is Irish. Only a few generations on this side of the Atlantic."

Michael's eyes crinkled at the corners, and he reached to run his fingertip across Nicky's nose. "Well, that explains the freckles."

That touch may have painted fire across his face, Nicky blushed so hard. Fucking pale skin. "You're one to talk, strawberry." He ruffled Michael's hair, what little of it there was.

The strands were crisp with hair product, and stuck at odd angles. Michael scowled as he rearranged it. "I'm not a redhead."

The vehemence in that statement made Nicky snicker. "Oh crap, you're self-conscious about it? But it's cute."

Michael arched an eyebrow. "Say that again?"

Though his stern expression was half-teasing, it still made Nicky hot under his clothes. "You're cute."

Heat flared in Michael's eyes, and if they hadn't been at a restaurant, Nicky was certain Michael would have grabbed him and kissed him until Nicky took it back, substituting *hot* or *sexy* or *very manly indeed* for "cute".

"You're going to pay for that later." Michael squeezed his side.

Their food came, so they settled into eating, chatting about their families and cars and motorcycles. Nicky learned that Michael had a much older sister who lived in Montana with a guy who did organic farming, so same as Nicky, Michael grew up as an only child. He learned that Michael's eyes rolled back with every bite he took of pizza.

Usually Nicky thought red wine tasted like vinegar and Sunday mass, but whatever Michael had ordered complemented the food so much that most of it was gone by the time they considered ordering dessert.

"I'm not really into sweets." Michael studied the menu.

That was okay. Nicky felt full and happy, and more than a little eager to get on to the next phase of his date. He'd been partially hard since they settled into their table. "Let's skip it." Nicky wondered if he had the guts to say what he was thinking. His palms felt damp, so he wiped them on his shorts.

Crap, was he seriously thinking of going back to Michael's place? If they were in an actual apartment, they could take off all their clothes before they got off. Hell, they could really...really...

Nicky didn't know if he was ready for that, but shit, between the past few days of hell with his mom, and the food and wine coursing through his system, he wanted to try it.

"How about we go to your place for dessert?" Nicky was amazed those words had come from his mouth.

"My place, huh?" That cocked eyebrow was back, together with a slow smile that made Nicky's boner go from half-hard to prepped-and-ready. "I can drive this time, right?"

Oh, shit. Nicky swallowed against the lump in his throat. Was that a suggestion? The kind of hint Nicky thought he'd been getting all night, and maybe before that? Or was it Nicky's nervousness making him imagine things? "Yeah, that's fine."

They split the check, which wasn't as expensive as Nicky had feared it would be, and made their way out of the restaurant and into the dark parking lot. Michael opened the car door for Nicky again. This time when that hand went to Nicky's lower back, Nicky couldn't help but tense.

He'd been cool with guys in the park grabbing his hips sometimes, but never lower to his ass. Funny, that probably made him some kind of prude. Michael would sure think so if Nicky mentioned it.

When Michael got in his side of the car and started the engine, he looked across the front seat and tilted his head. "Is something wrong?"

"No." Nicky couldn't make his voice calm.

Michael threw his arm across the seat to look over his shoulder and back out of the spot. "Is it about your mom?"

Maybe Nicky should have said yes to throw Michael off track, but he wasn't ready to start thinking about his mom quite yet. "No. Just thinking." Okay, that was it, the lead-in that could get them talking about what was running through his head.

"Thinking about what?"

"Well..." Nicky took a deep breath. Fuck it. He'd rather know what Michael expected to happen back at his place than find out when Michael bent him over. It wasn't even like Nicky would say no...necessarily. Heck, if Michael wanted Nicky to fuck him, it would be just as weird. Maybe weirder, because Nicky wasn't really thinking of Michael that way.

Of course, if he tried, maybe he could think of Michael like that...

"Are you a—?" Shit, he couldn't say *top or bottom* out loud. "I mean if we were to...would you want to..." Nicky focused on the road outside, the bridge passing by and the few boats on the canal below. "Forget about it. It's no big deal."

"It seems like a big deal." Michael's quick chuckle was only slightly louder than the road noise outside. "Am I a what?"

If Nicky got any more embarrassed, he'd burst into flames, so he went on the defensive. "Well, its seems like gay guys are all either..." *Top or bottom, top or bottom, top or bottom!* The thoughts rang through his head, but somehow the muscles of his throat seized whenever he tried to form the words. "And I just want to know which you are."

His frustration bled into annoyance, since Nicky was pretty sure Michael knew what he was getting at and was playing stupid. "We've gotten together a few times now, and we're going to your house. I don't think it's weird for me to want to know."

"Know what?" Michael winked at him across the front seat. Oh yeah. He knew exactly what was making Nicky squirm.

"Fine. Don't tell me." Nicky crossed his leg over his opposite knee, refusing to play the blushing virgin any longer. As much as he liked Michael's teasing, Nicky wasn't up for being made fun of.

"Aw. Don't pout." Michael drew up to a parking space painted red like a *No Parking* zone, but when Nicky read the sign, it turned out to be open to parking after eight on weekdays. Despite the tight squeeze, Michael managed to parallel park the Lincoln between a truck and an old Volkswagen Beetle that Nicky was surprised was still running.

Nicky reached for the door handle, wanting to get out of this conversation and on to finding out firsthand what Michael was expecting to do, but Michael grabbed Nicky's arm. The kiss Michael landed hit halfway between his cheek and his mouth.

"Are you asking if I like to fuck or be fucked?" Michael hooked a hand behind Nicky's neck and massaged his tight muscles.

Nicky's eyes were closed already, but he clamped them harder, nodding only once.

"What are you hoping I'll say?" Michael brushed his nose across Nicky's, in a move as sexy as it was comforting.

His pulse pounded in his ears, his dick beat in time in his shorts, and Nicky whispered the truth. "I don't know."

"Really? But I'd have thought..." Michael pulled back, his head tipped like he was confused and needed to read the real answer from Nicky's face. Then, all at once, Michael sealed his mouth to Nicky's, lips hot and wet and insistent. He plunged his tongue into Nicky's mouth, licking and nipping and biting on Nicky's bottom lip. "You are so fucking hot. You know that?"

Simple as the phrase was, Nicky's insides melted. If that was how Michael sounded—all growly and desperate—when he was about to fuck, then Nicky could take it. He could take anything to feel as wanted as he did right then. A gorgeous creature, sexy and as free as anything.

"If you want to bottom, I'll make it good for you. I swear." Michael roamed his hand down Nicky's back, hovering at that dip right above his Nicky's ass. "I mean—I'm versatile. I'd let you do me sometime if you wanted, but I have to admit, I'd really love to..."

Because it was dark in the car, and the street was empty, and Nicky was drunk on red wine and the taste of Michael's kisses, Nicky shifted farther into Michael's arms. He arched his back so the top curve of his ass drifted under Michael's hand. In between kisses, Nicky murmured, "Yeah. Me too."

Michael reached farther, so his fingers wrapped the underside of Nicky's butt cheek. The touch was incredibly intimate. More personal somehow than when a guy had his hand or mouth on Nicky's dick. Michael squeezed, growling his appreciation.

"How long do you have?" Michael took the keys out of the ignition and cracked open the car door. The interior light flooded the cabin.

Nicky looked at the screen of his phone. "Shit."

"Oh fuck, tell me you don't have to go soon." Michael sounded just as horny as Nicky felt. But between the light and the fact that there was only another half hour until his mom's home health aide needed to go home, Nicky flinched like he'd been doused in cold water.

"Yeah." Nicky gave his dick a quick rub. "I should have checked my phone. I knew Saundra could only stay two and a half hours, but..." How could Nicky explain he'd been having too much fun to think about time, and his responsibilities, and his life outside the world he was building with Michael?

"That's okay." Nicky would have expected Michael to be angry or at least annoyed, but Michael's expression was pure kindness. "You asked me to dinner and that's what we did. It's fine." Michael sounded like he was trying to get a handle on things, switch gears back to normal.

"I..." There were a lot of things Nicky wanted say. Like he'd had a great time or how he really, really hoped this meant they were moving toward dating. Heck, he may have said something about wanting to have sex, but the timer on his phone went off.

The last thing Nicky needed was to piss off Saundra by showing up late.

"Call me later. If you want." Michael got out of the car so fast Nicky couldn't read his expression. But the message was loud and clear. Michael was his to call. Like a boyfriend.

Nicky swallowed, trying to slow the racing of his heart.

"Good night." Michael handed him the keys.

Chapter Eight

"Are you okay?" His mother peered up at him, her forehead creased, though Nicky couldn't tell if it was because she was trying not to cough or because she was worried.

"Yeah. I'm fine." Nicky set the pile of folded boxes in the corner alcove. They looked wrong there, intruding as they were on his mom's sanctuary. Fitfully, Nicky tucked them under his arm and used the handhold to drag them back out into the hallway.

She wasn't expected to be at All Saints until evening the next day. Nicky could leave the cardboard reminders next to the staircase for the night.

"You don't seem fine." His mother coughed, and Nicky was worried she'd try to get up to follow him, so he rushed into the living room to make sure she stayed on the couch.

"There's just a lot to do." He wiped the sweat off his forehead. The chilled sheen under his clothes had more to do with his emotional state than the exercise he'd gotten hauling cardboard out of the back of the Lincoln. His brain ran a mile a minute, one second thinking he should convince his mom to stay, and another wondering if he should have gotten her a different doctor when she'd first received her diagnosis.

He couldn't even look at his mom, because Nicky was sure his eyes would betray his mixture of depression and panic. He dropped into the chair next to the couch, hand on his knee to stop it from bouncing.

"You should go out, Nicky. Take a break."

Nicky shook his head. He couldn't leave her alone. "I'm fine."

He could feel his mother's concern pouring off her, her gaze on his cheek as Nicky tried to focus on the sitcom reruns. "You could invite a friend over. I don't need you hovering over me."

She sounded as irritable as Nicky felt.

"Maybe." No way would he invite Cody or any of the guys from the station. The only person Nicky wanted to see was the one man he shouldn't invite to his home. But, dammit, now that Nicky had thought about seeing Michael, Nicky wanted it so badly he felt it in his teeth. "I guess I could give *someone* a call."

My boyfriend, his mind offered. *My boyfriend, who I'm crazy about and who's been calling me every night asking when we can get together.*

He couldn't say those things to his mom, and he didn't know why they popped into his head uninvited.

"You do that." His mother twisted on the couch, her eyelids fluttering like Nicky's stress was draining her energy. Nicky excused himself from the room and went upstairs to dial Michael's number with trembling fingers.

"Hey, sexy. What's up?"

Nicky rubbed the back of his neck. "Um...is your car still in the shop?"

There was noise in the background, like Michael was doing something in his apartment. "Yep. But I finally sucked it up and got a rental, why?"

"Any chance you'd be willing to come to my place?"

In the time it took Michael to answer, Nicky thought of a hundred ways this could go wrong. Even Michael saying no would hurt, since Nicky felt so brittle. He listened for a scoff that would mean Michael was offended.

In the end, Michael let out a long exhalation. "Nicky, I'm not trying to be contrary, but does your mom know you're gay?"

"No," Nicky said without reservation. He wasn't going to tell her. And for sure, not tonight, right when she was heading to the hospice center the next day. "She's sick, man." Nicky shouldn't have to explain, but he did anyway. "And religious, and—"

"So if I came over, what would happen?" Michael didn't sound distrustful so much as cautious. "We'd tell your mom I'm a friend of yours and then we'd go make out in your bedroom?"

"No...well, maybe." Nicky threw off his sweatshirt, suddenly too hot. The plan sounded ridiculous, and even juvenile. At the same time, Nicky needed not to be alone. "Though I guess if all you want is to fuck me, you may have to wait until I can get away."

Michael was silent on the other end for so long that Nicky wasn't sure whether he was still on the line. *Fuck.* Maybe Nicky had screwed up. If this was only sex, he could handle that...maybe. But Nicky needed something more in his life. At least right now.

"You want me to come over?" Michael's voice was quiet. Less strident than normal.

"Yeah." Nicky thought about offering food, or a blowjob, or even more if that's what it would take, but he didn't want to have to make deals or negotiations. Maybe it was too much to ask, but Nicky wanted Michael to come over just because Nicky wanted him to. "If you could."

This time, Michael's sigh was undeniable. Rife with frustration, perhaps, but also signaling that he was about to give in. "Fine. I've got a few things I have to wrap up here, but I should be over in around an hour."

Michael chopped the steamed broccoli with more force than he probably should have, and by the time he was done scrubbing the cutting board, he might have removed a layer of bamboo.

God, what in the hell was he doing?

With Mark, Michael had never been in this situation. Mark's paranoia about anyone suspecting he was gay meant Michael didn't meet any of Mark's family or friends.

After slicing the tofu and scooping the brown rice out of his rice cooker, Michael shook tamari and a few other seasonings over the casserole dish. Crap, he was even cooking for Nicky. This whole thing would crash and burn if Nicky woke up and realized he wasn't that gay after all.

Michael scrubbed down the counters and popped the sponge in the washing machine. He was in it now, and there was no turning back. Worst-case scenario, Michael would feel like an idiot and he and Nicky would go back to meeting in secret. Best-case scenario?

His imagination didn't stretch that far.

After fastening the lid on the baking dish, Michael gathered his backpack, keys and wallet. With a reluctant twitch of his lips, he went to the bathroom and grabbed his toothbrush and a few supplies. He had no reason to think he'd sleep over. Nicky hadn't invited him, and Michael couldn't guess where he'd sleep, but on the off chance Nicky's house was bigger than Michael imagined, it was best to plan ahead.

Outside, the rental car sat in innocuous silence among the older and more beat-up student cars. The Mazda hatchback wasn't fancy. In fact, he'd rented it as an economy car, but Michael had to admit it was nice that when he turned the key in the ignition, the car actually started.

The drive to Beacon Hill was an easy shot, and though Michael could have taken surface streets and been just fine, he got on the highway and let the engine open. Fine, he sped a little, but it had been so long since he'd been able to get on the highway and be certain he wouldn't break down.

A half hour later, Michael pulled up next to the address Nicky had given him. Paint chipped off the front of the house, and the tattered curtains hung in the picture window. Nicky's motorcycle was the only thing about the scene that was new and clean and shiny.

Michael texted Nicky, saying he was there. After all, Nicky may have changed his mind or decided he wanted to go somewhere with Michael instead. Maybe they'd head to some park, kiss and suck each other to oblivion without having to cross this uncomfortable step of Michael going inside Nicky's house.

The oddest thing was if they did that, Michael would be let down. He'd driven across town. *Fuck it.* They were doing this, even if Michael felt like an idiot after.

The door opened, and Nicky jogged down a set of front steps so rickety Michael wasn't sure they'd hold Nicky's weight. When Nicky grinned, Michael forgot his hesitations. All he could feel was happy.

"Hey." Michael closed the hatchback's door carefully so he didn't startle anyone inside. Amazingly, the door shut on his first try.

"Hey." Nicky came to a stop in front of him, gaze darting all over—down Michael's body, over Michael's face, like Nicky couldn't get enough of looking at him. "You came."

"Yeah." Michael wasn't sure why there was so much hope and fear written in Nicky's expression. He handed Nicky the casserole. "Uh, this isn't cooked yet, but if you have an oven..."

God, it was stupid to have brought food.

Nicky took a step closer, landing a grateful kiss on Michael's cheek. "I really appreciate it." He gestured with the casserole dish, but Michael was pretty sure he meant he appreciated that Michael had showed up. From the state of Nicky's browned and overgrown front yard, Michael had the sense that not many people visited.

"No worries. Are we going inside?"

"Sure." Nicky nodded toward the door, and then led the way up the steps. "Excuse the rotten parts. I was going to fix them, but then my mom came down with pneumonia..."

"It's okay." Michael hoped Nicky didn't spend all night self-conscious about where he lived.

The house was built like an old colonial, more common in this part of town than up by where Michael lived, and the front door led into an entryway with a set of stairs heading up the middle.

Straight ahead, Michael saw the white appliances and brighter lighting of a kitchen, while to the right was a doorway to a dark room with a television blaring.

"Come on." Nicky frowned, his gaze on the floor, but Michael did as Nicky asked, following him into what seemed to be a living room but had been outfitted with a hospital bed on the side. A woman sat on the couch, her hair thin under a skullcap and her skin sunken around her eyes.

"Oh, hello." She patted at the blanket over her lap, and then landed a hand on her cheek. "I'm sorry I'm such a mess. You must be Nicky's friend."

"Yes. Hi. I'm Michael." He went to where she was sitting. She didn't seem capable of getting up, so Michael reached out.

He could feel her bones through her skin as they shook hands, and he hoped she couldn't see him recoil. The room smelled stale, like cleaners were fighting with mold, or maybe that was just the normal odor of people who were as sick as Nicky's mother looked.

"This is my mom, Lydia," Nicky said from behind him.

Nicky's mom smiled. Her eyes were tired, creased around the edges in a way that seemed out of place with her features. She didn't look that old, and if Nicky was her son, she couldn't have been much over sixty.

"Hi, Lydia." Michael smiled, though it was hard to do when seeing her obviously pained face.

Her lips quirked up. "It's good of you to come around."

There was a lump in Michael's throat, filling the place he normally stored his righteous indignation. For some reason, he'd expected to be curt with this woman, or at the very least to think of her as the enemy.

Now that Michael was seeing her, he couldn't feel any kind of animosity. She was dying. There was no way not to notice.

"Michael brought dinner." Nicky held up the casserole pan.

Lydia made a face like a wince. "I'm not hungry."

Nicky *tsk*ed, rounding to where a side table held a lineup of medicine bottles with white caps. "Did you take these this afternoon?" He pulled out a couple pills and pushed them into his mother's hand.

His mother rolled her eyes. "I don't know why I bother. They don't work." She threw them back, frowning as she swallowed.

"Here." Michael picked her cup off the coffee table and handed it her direction. He'd never in his life been around someone this sick. All his grandparents were still alive, and the sole great-grandparent who'd passed away in his lifetime had lived out in Port Orchard, a place his parents only made him go a few times.

"Thank you." She took the cup in her shaking hand.

Michael wondered if he should help her get it to her lips, but she managed a sip without help.

"You boys don't have to stay." She waved them off with a quick gesture. "Go talk. Have fun."

Across the couch, Nicky's gaze met Michael's—his eyes going wider as if his mom had just said some kind of innuendo—and Michael cringed to think of what kind of fun he'd been coming here to have.

"Sure, Mom." Nicky crossed in front of her, landing an awkward kiss on her cheek as he passed. "And we'll bring you some food when it's done."

With how fast Nicky cleared out of the room and headed to the kitchen, Michael was surprised his mom had the reflexes to call out, "You don't need to. I'm not hungry."

That was an argument Michael wasn't planning to get in the middle of, so he followed into the kitchen in the back of the house. Unlike the living room, which felt like a shrine built out of religious statuary, the kitchen was wallpapered with a floral pattern. The windowsills were decorated with doodads in addition to planters and vases. But somehow in here, the effect of the mournful saints and baby angels wasn't quite as intense as in the living room.

"I probably should have warned you." Nicky set down the casserole dish and turned on the rickety oven.

"Oh. Well, I expected her to be sick. With what you said..." Seeing the expression of confusion in Nicky's eyes, Michael trailed off. Okay, maybe Nicky could have given Michael more preparation, but it's not like Nicky hadn't shared that she was going into end-of-life care. It was just a shock coming upon a person that—there was no other way to say it—was so close to *the end.*

Death was such a private matter, usually confined to hospitals or inside houses. Michael felt like he'd been let in on something intimate. About a hundred times more so than if he'd come over and he and Nicky had simply fucked.

"I mean about the religion thing." Nicky wiped his hands on his jeans like he was embarrassed. "I don't notice it anymore. She got a bunch of the stuff when her own mom died, but then it started multiplying in the last few years..." He scrubbed a hand through his hair, and then on the back of his neck. The skin there had faded to pink.

Michael guessed Nicky hadn't had much time lately to motorcycle in the sun. "Oh. That." He shrugged. His own mom had weird crap all over the place, though in her case it was more likely to be plants, dream catchers and statues of Shiva. "I figured you were religious or something, and that's why you never..." He didn't want to say *came out of the closet.* Even with the television cranked to a level they practically had to shout over, Michael didn't want to be overheard.

"I'm not religious." Nicky went to the fridge and got out two beers. He handed one to Michael and opened the other for himself.

"Okay." Michael downed a measure to have something to do with his hands. "You know, you don't need to explain anything to me."

Nicky glanced sideways, his lips pinching. "Like hell I don't."

The remark cut so fast that Michael couldn't figure out where it came from. He gritted his teeth, trying not to rise to the bait. "What do you mean by that?"

"Nothing." Nicky rubbed his face, hanging his head and looking small, like maybe he'd shrunk recently. "It's just, I know what you need. What you want me to do if we're going to…"

Michael thought about stopping Nicky, telling him that tonight Michael didn't need anything from him at all. But he wanted to hear this, to know how things looked between them from Nicky's perspective.

"I can't be like that right now." Nicky's chest deflated. "Hell, I can't even be a regular person. Do regular shit like go to work or to the store without worrying. And I have to pack her stuff up tomorrow…" He swallowed, eyes wide open and his gaze a bottomless pit of need. "But, I want you here. I can't offer you anything, but I want you here so much."

Michael crossed the kitchen in a few steps and grabbed Nicky around the shoulders. He didn't worry about Nicky's mom out in the living room, or anyone seeing through the pitch-black windows, because what Nicky needed right now was a friend. No matter what Michael might want in the future, he could be a friend for Nicky. The guy who held him and patted his back, letting him shudder and maybe cry a little.

"Hey. It's okay." Michael rubbed Nicky over his short-sleeved shirt, not letting their skin touch, because if that happened, Michael would want to give Nicky a kiss. "It's fine. Just relax." In the week since they'd last seen each other, Nicky seemed to have grown more fragile. "Let's have another beer, huh?"

Nicky's shoulders bounced on a laugh. "Okay." He wiped his face, pulling away. They were only a third of the way through their bottles, but he grabbed another two out of the fridge. With a sly smirk, he said, "We should tip into my mom's schnapps collection."

"Oh. It's going to be that kind of party." Michael sidled up next to Nicky, wanting like anything to touch him but settling for a hip bump. "Peach schnapps out of dusty bottles? Yum." As much as Michael hated sweet drinks, he'd share a glass with orange juice if it kept the smile on Nicky's face.

"No. Peppermint." The way Nicky shuddered made it clear that he didn't like schnapps any more than Michael did. "But we'd have to give Mom a nip. I swear she can smell that stuff like a bloodhound."

The idea that the frail woman on the couch in the living room was a secret party girl tickled Michael's imagination. "What could it hurt?" Actually, Michael had no idea what could go wrong for Nicky's mother mixing small amounts of alcohol with her medications, but he figured Nicky would know well enough what his mother could handle.

"Yeah." Nicky went over to a cabinet. Inside was a surprisingly well-stocked liquor cabinet, though the bottles looked like they'd been there for a decade. When he rounded with the schnapps in hand, Nicky's face had softened. "What did you say was in that casserole?"

"Tofu and broccoli. Some brown rice and a little organic cheese." Michael should have had something better to offer. If they were getting decadent, his casserole wasn't exactly helping.

Nicky tilted his head, his expression serious. "And would you say peppermint is the best accompaniment to broccoli tofu casserole, or should we try blackberry?"

Michael barked out a laugh, surprised Nicky had gotten one over on him. "Oh man, I can't imagine which is worse. Could I stick with beer?"

"Suit yourself," Nicky said with deadpan humor. "I think you'll be missing out."

Michael couldn't resist touching him, just for a second. He meant to poke Nicky's side, but it turned into a rub. Michael curled his fingers around taut muscle, but only long enough to feel Nicky squirm. "No I won't." Quickly, so as not to freak Nicky out, he blew him a kiss.

Chapter Nine

Nicky would have thought dinner would be uncomfortable, what with him and Michael sitting on chairs next to his mom on the couch, watching old episodes of *Law and Order* and eating off plates on their laps, but it was fun. His mom managed a few bites, not even complaining that the food involved tofu. If anything, Nicky suspected she chewed and swallowed easier than she could have meat.

Afterwards, they each drank a thimbleful of his mom's favorite schnapps, and though Michael winced like he'd taken medicine, Nicky's mom smiled. "Nicky Senior likes to cook," she told Michael. Her eyes sparkled, and it seemed like she thought Nicky's father was still alive. Or maybe he felt real to her because soon they'd be reunited.

"You know what they say about a man who likes to cook?" Michael waggled his eyebrows.

Nicky's mouth dropped open. Was Michael flirting with his mother?

"I don't believe I do." His mother's chuckle turned into a cough.

Michael shrugged, making it clear he didn't really have a punch line. "They have big spatulas?"

His mom giggled, maybe the slightest bit tipsy from the schnapps, but Nicky thought most of her good humor was from having company.

Michael cleared the dishes while Nicky got his mom ready for bed in the living room. She surprised Nicky by mentioning, once he was tucking her in, what a nice man Michael was.

He kissed her forehead and went into the bathroom to wash his hands. Michael had finished up in the kitchen and was fussing with the countertops and reorganizing the refrigerator.

"Thanks for cleaning." Nicky came up behind him, wanting to give Michael a hug but not knowing whether Michael would accept it after so much forced "just friends" behavior.

"No worries." Michael turned so his back was to the counter and reached for Nicky's hand. Pulling Nicky close, he pecked a kiss on Nicky's cheek. "Your mom's nice."

Nicky went into his embrace. "Yeah. Well, she's my mom." There'd been times as a kid he'd shouted at her, or as a teen when he'd stormed upstairs and slammed his door. In adulthood, he'd let himself blame her sometimes for his confusion over his sexuality. But when it came down to it, she'd always made sure he had food to eat and clothes to wear. She'd put Band-Aids on his scraped knees and baked him white cake with chocolate icing just how he liked on his birthday.

It was hard to take seriously those times when she'd lost her temper and yelled, or slapped him, in light of everything. Now that he was losing her, none of that mattered. She'd been his everything when he was small. Soon he wouldn't have her, not even to blame.

"Yeah. I know." Michael hugged Nicky, breath ruffling in his ear, strong arms making sure Nicky was safe.

"Man, this is the worst date ever. I'm sorry I made you come." Nicky tried to laugh off his discomfort. There was no point in getting dragged into depression. He had tomorrow for that, and the next day.

"Nah. It's fine." Michael rubbed Nicky's arms, setting him back so they could both get themselves together. "Do you want me to go now, or stick around for a while? We could watch a movie or something."

Nicky considered it. "Yeah. I guess." It wasn't ten yet, and he certainly didn't plan to go to sleep in the next couple hours. "Unless you have to be somewhere early tomorrow."

"I don't have to be at work until eleven."

"Cool." Even if his mother hadn't been asleep in the living room, Nicky couldn't have watched TV in there. Despite the hundreds of channels on its TV, that room had become his mom's long ago. "You mind watching something upstairs? It'd have to be on my computer, but I have a few DVDs."

"That would be fine. Or we could use mine." Michael nodded over to his messenger bag, where Nicky guessed he had a laptop stored.

Nicky grinned. "You brought a computer on a date?" Nicky shouldn't even be calling it that, considering they'd just had dinner with his mother, but it still struck Nicky as funny.

"That and a toothbrush." Though Michael's wink as well as the toothbrush comment were suggestive, Nicky found Michael's preparedness endearing.

He'd bet Michael had lube and condoms stored in that hefty-looking bag as well. Along with tissues, antibacterial soap and quite possibly a Swiss army knife. "What's your screen size?"

"Fifteen inches," Michael said with enough pride that Nicky might have thought he was boasting about something more private. "How about yours?"

Nicky's cheeks got hot. No way was he getting into that kind of pissing match, so he opted to say, "Yours is probably newer anyway. Let's go up to my room."

Tiptoeing might have been a strong word for how they climbed the stairs to the second floor, but Nicky didn't want to wake his mother. He and Michael crammed into Nicky's small space, Michael landing on Nicky's bed immediately since there wasn't anywhere else to sit.

"Is it okay that I'm up here?" Michael folded one clean and manicured foot under him. Nicky had never thought he'd be attracted to a man's feet, but he could imagine kissing each of Michael's toes.

"Yeah. It's fine." His mother had never minded who Nicky had in his room, even in high school when he'd tried to be interested in girls. "As long as we don't watch too loud."

He eyed the bed, unsure where to sit, but that only lasted for a second because there were no other options.

"So." Nicky dropped onto his mattress, gathering his legs up.

"What kind of things do you like to watch?" Michael pulled a sleek MacBook out of his bag and opened it. Considering that the car Michael normally drove was a hunk of junk, Nicky was surprised Michael had such a drool-worthy piece of tech hidden in his bag.

He opened a browser and then Netflix, and the list of recommendations included every one of *The Fast and the Furious* movies.

"Oh, man. You like those too?" Nicky leaned forward to better see the titles. He loved the movies, though the tragedy with the film's star cast a dark shadow. "Can you believe about Paul Walker? So messed up."

Michael rubbed Nicky's shoulder. "Sorry. I'll look for a comedy." He reached to click the keys, but Nicky urged his hand away.

"Nah. It's okay. I mean, it's too bad, but I still like the movies." He shoved away the hint of sadness he felt. No need to let a Hollywood tragedy get in the way of watching high-speed car chases. "You know, I never saw the fifth one of these." Nicky pointed to the icon. "You interested?"

Michael grabbed a handful of Nicky's ass and gave it a playful squeeze. "Of course." He brushed a kiss across Nicky's jaw before turning back to the computer. "We can watch anything you want." The movie started up and Michael set it on the dresser across from the bed.

Nicky stacked his pillows against the headrest, and for the opening scene he and Michael tried to sit shoulder to shoulder, but it quickly became apparent that they were too cramped.

"Hey, move like this..." Michael pushed Nicky in front of him, which Nicky would have thought would block Michael's view until Michael urged Nicky to lie against his chest.

"I'm going to crush you." Nicky looked behind him in concern.

"We'll change positions if it gets uncomfortable." Michael pulled Nicky back so he sat in the cradle of Michael's splayed legs. He rested his chin on Nicky's shoulder and his arms around Nicky's waist.

Truth be told, it wasn't the most comfortable position, and Nicky was pretty sure he was in fact crushing Michael, but it felt so good to be close together that Nicky stayed like that through the beginning of the movie.

As with all of the movies in this franchise, revving engines and accelerating cars dominated practically every scene. Nicky had a stiffie within the first ten minutes, especially since at every spinout Michael squeezed like they were leaning into a turn.

When Nicky bent forward to give Michael a chance to stretch, Michael massaged Nicky's shoulders.

Maybe Michael was doing it as a foray into something physical, but Nicky couldn't bring himself to call Michael on it. Those long-fingered hands felt too good. Nicky still exercised most days, but limited gym time meant he hadn't stretched in a week. His muscles felt like too-taut strings on a guitar, being plucked and played under Michael's fingertips.

"Hey, take off your shirt." Michael urged the fabric up Nicky's back.

"I knew you were trying to make a move." Nicky wasn't mad. If anything, he couldn't stop smiling as he pulled his shirt off and leaned forward in a blatant request for more massage.

"Hey, now. I'm just being nice." Michael was a liar, since he took his own shirt off as well. He stroked and rubbed Nicky's back, hard enough to get into the fibers and loosen Nicky's nerves.

"Gugnh." Nicky grunted. "Fuck, can I fall in love with you now?" Nicky shouldn't have said that. But shit, right then he would have given a lot for him and Michael to be on the same page with their feelings, on wanting to spend more time together.

"Who could blame you?" Michael asked in a cheeky voice. He scooted forward until he was flush against Nicky's back.

Michael's erection was an unmistakable suggestion, one that made Nicky's cock pulse with fullness.

"Don't you want to keep watching the movie?" Nicky held his breath as he waited for the answer. Nicky needed Michael to touch him and make him feel good, but the last thing in the world he'd do was say it out loud and risk scaring Michael off.

Michael drifted his touch up Nicky's sides, and then around to his nipples to tweak. In the background, engines screamed. Nicky's breath rushed out in a low, almost silent growl.

"We can watch and do other things." To prove his point, Michael reached between Nicky's legs.

"Yeah?" Normally the two of them negotiated ahead of time, and with his mom downstairs, it seemed like exactly the type of situation where Nicky should put down limits.

But the weirdest thing was Nicky didn't want to. He wanted Michael to lead, so Nicky wouldn't have to think.

"Come over here." With a gentle push, Michael got Nicky lying on his side and spooned him.

Michael's knees fit right behind Nicky's and their hips lined up so Nicky could feel the heat radiating off Michael's stiffness even through however many layers of fabric. With arms around Nicky's waist and lips on Nicky's neck, Michael ground tight, his cock riding the crease of Nicky's ass.

"Oh God," Nicky whispered. Michael's hand had found its way between Nicky's legs. Not stroking so much as squeezing and pressing. Adding the same pressure Nicky could feel on his tailbone.

For minute after long minute, Michael rolled them like that. Deep friction and nothing more. Nicky's skin tingled everywhere it touched Michael's, and he shivered from the feel of Michael's sparse chest hair between his shoulder blades. But with him wearing jeans, and Michael in some kind of thick camping material, it felt like they were trapped in a vise from the waist down.

"You want to try this with less clothes?" Michael's murmur shivered down Nicky's neck, over his chest and to the place where he was trapped humping helplessly into Michael's palm.

"I'd feel weird getting all the way naked." Nicky rushed for his belt, though. If they were doing this, it had to be fast. Quick and hot, and too rushed for him to worry that his mom might wake up and need his attention.

"That's fine." Michael fumbled with his pants, and Nicky pushed his own down. Michael got them right where they were before, Michael riding his crease, but this time Michael's bare cock met nothing but skin.

"Mmm..." Michael's quiet moan said everything Nicky was thinking.

Nicky could feel Michael's precome between the cheeks of his ass, Michael's cock sliding deeper and deeper until it was right...there. Friction right above Nicky's asshole. How had Nicky not realized having a thick weight pressed there would feel so good?

He arched his back, trying to get more.

"Can I get some lube out?" Michael reached behind him for his messenger bag.

Nicky didn't care if Michael fucked him. Everything he did with Michael was better than Nicky expected. Michael clicked the light off next to the bed as he cuddled once again against Nicky's back.

"Hey." Michael craned his head around, landing a kiss close enough to Nicky's mouth that Nicky got the hint and reciprocated.

The kiss was furtive but full of the smile he could feel on Michael's lips. A wet hand covered Nicky's dick, smooth and warm, and Nicky bit his lip so he wouldn't gasp.

"I'm not going to fuck you, okay?"

Nicky might have voiced disagreement over that if he wasn't shocked into silence by the feel of lube being slicked all along his crack. Michael's fingers were quick, teasing. Oh God, they were...he was touching... Nicky squirmed, not sure whether he was trying to get closer or farther away. That probing fingertip was stroking, tapping, dipping into the center just far enough for Nicky to feel a twinge of totally unfamiliar sensation.

Nicky whispered every curse word he could imagine and some that weren't words at all. Without a doubt, Nicky wanted those fingers inside him.

"You like?" Michael settled his cock into that slick furrow he'd created. He pressed kisses into Nicky's shoulder, pulling back before pushing forward. Michael changed his position so he thrust his cock head into the space below Nicky's balls. "Oh yeah." Michael drew out, then thrust into that space, creating friction and heat and a tightness even Nicky could feel since his thighs were trapped by his shorts. "This is okay, right?"

"Yeah, but..." Nicky bit his lip to stop himself from saying the words on his mind. *Fuck me, fuck me, fuck me...* The chorus sang through his mind, but Nicky knew enough from his research to realize Michael couldn't just slip inside him. There'd be preparation, and probably getting out a condom, and Nicky didn't want any of that. He needed Michael to keep holding him close, whispering in his ear.

"Yeah?" Michael slowed what he was doing, as if he was listening very carefully for what Nicky might want.

"Could you do it the other way again?" Nicky tried to figure out a way to describe it without having to resort to either hand gestures or saying out loud *between the cheeks of my ass instead of between my legs.* "Can you get off that way?"

"You mean like this?" Michael shifted his hips, until he was back so the base of him rubbed along Nicky's crack.

Nicky hoped his sigh wasn't too obvious. "Yeah. Like that. Can you?"

"I think so." Michael rolled them so Nicky was underneath and Michael was laid out on top.

The position felt right, safe, even though anyone who walked in would assume Michael was fucking him. Then Michael thrust, a smooth pressure right along his crease, so deep it felt like Michael was inside him already, and Nicky forgot to think. He forgot to do anything but arch off the bed.

"Fuck, Nicky..." Michael was everywhere, all around him, nipping and kissing and stroking his whole body over Nicky's shoulders and hips and legs. The only place he wasn't anymore was on Nicky's dick, since in this position Michael needed his hands to hold him up. "Squeeze me."

After a second of processing what Michael was asking, Nicky clenched his butt cheeks.

"God... Yeah... Just like that..." The tension in Michael's body was so hot Nicky couldn't help but get a hand under his hips and grab his dick. He scrunched a shirt underneath him, tensing. Despite being close to the end, they still moved in short, jerky, almost silent motions, the hint of the bed creaking the only sound that could give them away.

"You'd want it like this?" Michael's murmurs tickled Nicky's ear.

Not lifting his head, Nicky nodded. God, he wanted everything. The kisses and the hot breath. The smell of musk and end-of-the-day sweat. Even the movie in the background making this seem like the most natural thing in the world. "Yeah. Want it so bad."

Wetness splashed on Nicky's lower back, and Michael's thrusts got sloppier and slicker.

"Your finger," Nicky panted. He wanted to feel it for a second. Just to see what it was like. He pushed up to his knees, ass sticking out to meet Michael's slowing rubs.

"I..."

Nicky figured Michael was going to balk about germs or whatever, but Nicky didn't care. Hell, if Michael had wanted to, Nicky would have let Michael fuck him raw that night. "C'mon. Do it. I want to know."

Michael's touch was there, a single finger rubbing through lube and sweat, so slippery Nicky would have thought his digit would have sank right inside, but though that first press reached what Nicky assumed was a knuckle, something stopped it from going any farther.

"It's okay." Michael landed a warm hand on Nicky's back—a move soothing and firm at the same time—and pressed past whatever clenched muscle in Nicky's body was holding him out.

The feeling was like having the wind knocked out of him. Sharp and intense and making him hold his breath while he struggled to reconcile what he'd expected with what he felt.

"It's a little weird at first." Slowly, Michael withdrew his fingertip, only to press inside again. This time, he moved more easily, though Nicky could tell that one quick clench of his muscles would grab hold of Michael's hand.

It was a weird feeling, letting Michael enter him. Not only because the pain was as acute as the pleasure, but also because Nicky had to keep loose, pressing back against Michael to allow Michael's touch inside.

"You want me to stop?" Another gentle press inward, slicking more lube and possibly come into Nicky's body, setting off nerves that Nicky hadn't known he had.

"No." Nicky sped up his hand on his dick. He'd thought coming like this would be challenging, trying to relax when all his body wanted to do was tense. But as soon as he started the climb, the feeling of something inside him turned so sweet it was all he could do not to howl and buck back into Michael's searching hand.

"Oh fuck, oh fuck, oh..."

Michael dragged him up until Nicky was sitting on Michael's finger, but Michael put a hand across Nicky's mouth, whispering in his ear, "Shhhhhhh, Nicky. Don't scream."

Well, fuck, that only made Nicky want to scream more. Michael's digit was dancing inside him, wiggling across nerve endings fit to burst from excitement.

"I'd finish you in my mouth, but I don't think you'd be able to keep quiet."

The picture of that flashed through Nicky's mind—his dick disappearing between Michael's lips as Michael pressed something, anything, deep into Nicky's ass—and Nicky came apart in a thousand pieces. His insides jerked, exploding, all the more so because he held as still as he could, Michael against his back and Michael's fist in his mouth, while lights danced behind Nicky's eyes and his sinews struggled to break free of their fastenings.

He was flying. Untethered. Totally free and in orbit. All the better because Michael had a hold on him and wasn't letting go.

"Oh my God." The way Michael said it was a lot closer to "ohmigod", making him sound ten years younger and a different gender from the guy Nicky had in his bed. "Don't move."

Nicky didn't think he could. But when Michael let go of him, it occurred to Nicky that what Michael meant was *don't flop on the bed face first and fall asleep like you want to right now.* If Michael hadn't gotten back armed with tissues and wet wipes a second later, Nicky probably would have just collapsed and slept in a mess of come and lube. Michael swept soft paper around Nicky's belly, under his balls, and then up along his crack.

The bath would have seemed embarrassing, possibly even humiliating, if Michael didn't murmur sexily the whole time.

"Fuck, I'm so tired." Nicky couldn't bring himself to tell Michael how good it had been. After all, it seemed like Michael already knew.

"Yeah. I figured." Michael smacked a kiss on Nicky's jaw. His words were smug, but Nicky figured he had a right to sound satisfied.

"Shit. I should check on my mom." Nicky fell onto his sheets, closing his eyes.

"I'd do it for you, but that would be creepy." Michael hovered, sitting on the bed.

"Yeah. Too creepy. But thanks." With a groan, Nicky rolled up to stand. He grabbed his shirt off the floor and pulled it on, unsure what to say to Michael, who seemed on the verge of leaving now that they'd finished fooling around. The credits were rolling on the movie, and if there was a time for Nicky to act, it was now before Michael did what he always did and took over. "You want to stay? One of us would have to sleep on the floor, but I could bring up cushions from the couch."

The way Michael bit the edge of his nail was uncharacteristic, and after a breath or two, Michael glowered at his hand, shaking it out like he could erase the nervous gesture. "I guess. I mean, if you need help packing tomorrow."

"Really?" Possibly Michael was using packing as an excuse, but Nicky didn't care. He'd love not to be alone when he started piling his mother's things in boxes. "That would be awesome."

A grin tilted Michael's lips, as if he were on even ground now that he had something concrete he could do.

Nicky would let Michael organize the whole damn process if it would keep Michael there.

"So, uh...I should just wait up here?" Michael's hand drifted back to his mouth, an unconscious gesture Nicky tried to ignore.

"Yeah. Though there's only the one bathroom downstairs. Er...use it whenever you're ready." Nicky put a hand on Michael's arm. "Hey." He searched Michael's face, wondering if Michael would pull away when all Nicky wanted to do was get closer. "Thanks. For everything."

Michael's smile was genuine, so Nicky pecked Michael on the cheek and slipped downstairs to make sure his mother was comfortable in her sleep.

Chapter Ten

Considering that Michael had been the one to bring a toothbrush, he shouldn't have felt so awkward when he woke up the next morning. Staring at the ceiling, he heard the sound of a shower downstairs. Sunlight streamed through the window, providing backlight for the bits of dust that floated in the air. Nothing in the house was dirty...exactly. But the whole place needed a massive decluttering. Maybe Nicky would go for it once he started packing his mother's things.

The door cracked open. "Hey. Good morning." Nicky came in, towel wrapped around his hips and torso dripping with water that fell from the tips of his hair. With his muscle-packed shoulders and his narrow waist and that ass that swelled out from those two dimples on his lower back, he could have been drawn from one of Michael's fevered jerk-off fantasies.

"Good morning." Michael pushed up to his elbows, blinking the sleep and anxiety from his eyes. Nicky wasn't some kind of test, and he wasn't purposely tricking Michael into a relationship. He was just a confused guy.

Anyway, Nicky was coming out...eventually. He'd started already when they'd gone to the restaurant together.

"D'you sleep okay?" Michael looked skeptically at the cushions still lined up on the floor and the tattered blanket twisted on top.

"Yeah." The flush on Nicky's face may have been from the shower, but when he bent to kiss Michael's cheek, Michael had a feeling he was embarrassed. "How about you?"

Michael didn't want to mention the tossing and turning, the thoughts he'd had all night about how he'd have to go into work that morning pretending nothing had happened—because hell if he'd tell Jesse he was dating Nicky if Nicky was introducing Michael as a friend.

"You know, you don't have to help pack, right?" Nicky slipped on his briefs under his towel.

"No, it's fine. Like I said, I've got a few hours before I have to work." Michael's insides were screaming at him to get out of there. At the very least to go pick up breakfast so he'd have some control over what he was eating—but if worse came to worst, he could always eat leftovers.

"You can take a shower if you like." Nicky flat-out blushed now, though why, Michael couldn't guess. "My mom's up already."

"Oh." Michael had forgotten that staying over might mean using the same bathroom as Nicky's mother. Talk about weird. "Yeah. That would be great."

"I put a fresh towel on the rack."

With a nod, Michael set off for the bathroom downstairs. He'd seen it the night before, but in low light and with his eyes half closed as he brushed his teeth. A few prints decorated the walls, and there were fewer knickknacks than elsewhere in the house. Sunlight cut across the white walls, giving the room a feeling that might be antiseptic if it weren't for the effigies trying to shove religion down Michael's throat.

The shower's water pressure left a lot to be desired. Michael washed away any residue from the day before and dried off with Nicky's threadbare towel. Since Michael had been old enough to care about politics, he'd been in favor of healthcare reform, but he'd never seen firsthand how an illness could wipe out a family's finances.

He hoped Nicky was doing okay on that front, because supporting a sick relative couldn't have been easy.

Nicky knocked on the door. "Hey, do you need to borrow some clothes?"

"Um..." Michael would be swimming in Nicky's shirts, but he could probably fit his underwear well enough. "Maybe." He didn't want to say *underwear* out loud, so he opened the door a few inches, murmuring, "Some briefs?"

Nicky's smile was infectious, the bounce in his posture at odds with how Michael felt poised on pins and needles. "Here. This stuff is from high school, so it might fit."

Michael wished there was a way to tell Nicky he didn't want to wear whatever fashion disasters Nicky had been up to ten years ago, but he accepted the clothes anyway. "They're going to be too short," he grumbled, because Michael didn't like having his physique compared to a high schooler's.

"They're shorts." Nicky frowned, like he'd picked up on Michael's negative mood. "But you don't have to wear them. If you want to just stick to the briefs..."

"I'm sure they'll be fine." Michael forced his mouth into a smile, finding that once it got there, his mood lifted. Nicky was trying. The least Michael could do was to try too. "Just give me a sec to get these on."

The shorts were simple cargoes, and a little tight, which had Michael flattered that Nicky had thought he was so thin. The shirt stretched across Michael's shoulders, making him somehow look gayer than he normally did, despite the Mariners logo on the front. Feeling awkward, he stepped out of the bathroom.

"Oh." Nicky gave Michael a once-over, his mouth dropping open. "Wow."

Michael couldn't help but laugh. He didn't normally dress in clothes this small unless he was going to a club. Doing so in Nicky's house felt like he had a giant flashing sign above his head screaming *I'm gay!*

"Too tight?" Michael lifted an eyebrow.

"Uh, no. Not at all." The bulge forming in the front of Nicky's pants told a different story.

If it weren't for the boxes Nicky had piled in the hallway—and Nicky's mother, and everything else—Michael would have been out of those clothes in the time it took to say, *Let's fuck.* As it was, Michael just patted Nicky's shoulder on his way to grab some boxes. "So, what all are we packing? Start upstairs or down?"

"Oh. Um...?" Nicky rubbed his neck, his eyes widening like he was getting ready to panic.

"Well, how about we get some coffee, and then you and her can decide what you want to do?"

"Yeah." Nicky nodded absentmindedly. "Yeah, okay. I have coffee. It's regular, and we only have whole milk."

"It's fine." Michael touched his arm, realizing exactly how much the prospect of moving was stressing Nicky out. "We'll do it together." This, Michael could handle. It was simple, finite. Unemotional.

"Okay." Instead of turning for the kitchen, Nicky headed for the living room, so Michael followed. He may as well say hi to Nicky's mother, since he'd be interacting with her things all morning.

Lydia sat on the couch, a small plate of half-eaten eggs on the table in front of her.

"Good morning." Michael gave her a wave.

"Oh, good morning." Nicky's mom smiled faintly. "Nicky said you'd slept over." She was back in her regular spot on the couch. If anything, she looked frailer and more tired than the night before.

Guilt hit Michael, confusing him since he had no idea what he felt bad about. Michael had long since gotten over shame about being gay, and he and Nicky were grown men. Still, he felt like he was at Nicky's house under false pretenses.

"Yeah. Uh...but he slept on the floor." Michael looked away, directing his attention down the hall to the kitchen where Nicky was fixing coffee. He couldn't believe he was making excuses. Like he was a teenager or something.

"He must have. I've been telling Nicky for ages to get a bigger bed. A man his size can barely fit in a tiny bed like that. What about when he wants to bring a girl around?"

Those words stabbed Michael in the gut. What was he supposed to do? Smile and nod? Agree with her? "Uh...I think I need some coffee." He made his way down the hallway, trying to erase the image of her well-meaning smile from his mind.

In the kitchen, Nicky was busy putting milk and sugar into a couple cups of coffee. Head down, he handed one to Michael, and Michael had a good idea that Nicky had overheard his mother.

"Thanks." Michael took a sip, opting not to say anything. He could demand Nicky go out there and tell his mom, but given that she was obviously hardcore religious, that knowledge might be enough to finish her off.

"I really appreciate your help with this, by the way." Nicky got some cereal out of a cabinet, his moves twitchy. "I know..." He set the box on the counter, where he'd already put some milk, bowls and spoons. "I know this isn't the easiest thing for you."

If Nicky didn't look so damn miserable right then, Michael would have railed that Nicky was putting him through the wringer, but there were dark circles under Nicky's eyes. Michael was pretty sure Nicky's exhaustion wasn't only from sleeping on the floor.

"It's okay." Michael winced on a large swallow of coffee, steeling himself. He'd promised to help pack—to be a friend. He wouldn't go back on that now. "I mean...you know I can't deal long-term with..." Michael shook his head, sitting down to grab some cereal. "Let's just worry about today, all right?"

Nicky nodded. "Yeah." The way he smiled took away a lot of Michael's reservations. Nicky looked at Michael like Michael was the answer to everything he ever wanted.

Michael would deal with more than random comments from Nicky's mother if it meant putting that light in Nicky's eyes. "So, where do you want to start?" He shoveled the cereal in his mouth, wanting to get as much done as possible before his shift at the coffee shop.

"I guess here is as good as anywhere." Nicky started going through the cabinets in between bites of cereal.

Surreptitiously, Michael folded the first of the small boxes. Nicky didn't put too many things on the kitchen table for Michael to wrap in packing paper. Just a few cups—two for tea and a few plastic tumblers, the kind you got at airports or in tourist shops. They said Las Vegas, Disneyland, Orlando, Dallas, and Michael was tempted to ask when Nicky's mother had taken the trips and whether Nicky had gone along. Given Nicky's fragile emotional state, Michael thought it best to wait.

They'd gotten through the kitchen by the time they'd finished their second cup of coffee. In the hallway, he and Nicky folded a few more boxes, stretching the packing tape across the bottom. "So. The living room next?"

"I dunno." Nicky rubbed the back of his neck.

Michael would have thought that getting started would calm Nicky down, but apparently not. From his back pocket, Michael pulled out his phone to check the time. Shit, he really should leave soon if he was going to make it to work.

Maybe he could call in sick, or at least late. He'd never done that before, not once in the years he'd worked at Speedy Coffee, but this wasn't some hangover or poor planning on his part. This was helping out a friend.

Nicky's mom started coughing, a wet, hacking, gasping sound unlike the gentler ones from the night before. Nicky kicked his way past boxes and rushed to his mom's side.

"You okay, Ma?" Nicky fumbled for something half-hidden behind the couch. From what seemed like out of nowhere, he pulled a tube that Michael now realized was attached to a rolling canister of oxygen. "Here." Nicky put a mask to his mom's face, covering her nose and mouth.

But the coughing continued. Ragged...painful...until it clawed at Michael's guts and made him want to do anything to make it stop.

"Um...I'm going to see if I can get someone to cover my shift." Michael backed out of the room. His heart pounded, thrumming in his chest. This was real. Nicky's mom hadn't seemed the picture of health the night before, but at that moment Michael wondered if he was supposed to call an ambulance or keep packing. The uncertainty made him feel hollowed out. Nauseated, but knowing that if he disappeared to the bathroom to be sick, he'd create a whole other thing for Nicky to deal with.

Michael slipped out the back door into the stark and empty yard. One ear listening for the volume and frequency of Nicky's mom's coughing, he dialed Jesse's number.

On the third ring, Jesse picked up, slightly out of breath. "Hey. What's up?"

The list of things that were up was too long to get into, but at least the volume of coughs from inside had settled down. "Um...listen." Michael wasn't sure he'd ever felt this uncertain in his life. Usually he was in control of what he took on. He chose and planned, plotted and carried out. He was careful not to get sucked into things where he'd feel powerless. "I have a friend..." Great, now he was referring to Nicky as a friend too. "His mom is really sick, and he needs help today."

"Wait...oh hell no. You're not bailing on me!"

Michael gritted his teeth. He couldn't blame Jesse for being annoyed, but if Jesse were here—if he'd heard Nicky's mom coughing or seen the stricken expression on Nicky's face—he wouldn't dismiss Michael's need for a personal day. "I don't need the whole day off." That's what Michael wanted, though he'd settle for just a few hours. "Maybe Sheila can cover for a while. I wasn't even on until eleven."

"She's not here yet." Jesse sounded distracted, like maybe he was making someone's order, and then a crashing noise carried over the line, like Jesse had dropped the phone.

"Fucker." Michael rubbed his jaw, glad of his beard, which meant he didn't look any worse for wear from not having shaven. "Well, call me when Sheila comes in. I'll get in touch with Henri. I don't think he works today. Maybe he could relieve you in the afternoon."

"Fine. Whatever." Jesse's answer was snapped, but Michael knew him too well to think Jesse would stay angry.

In the time it had taken Michael to finish the call, Nicky appeared at the back door. He stepped outside, face pale, and didn't say a word before curling into Michael's arms.

Nicky's shoulders hunched as he shook. Michael didn't know if Nicky actually shed any tears, but he wouldn't have blamed Nicky if he had. Michael barely knew Nicky's mother, and he was torn up around her.

He held Nicky with one arm, and with the other hand, Michael scrolled through to Henri's number. Henri hadn't worked at Speedy Coffee all summer, but he was the only person in the world besides Michael, Sheila and Jesse who knew how to work Speedy's register.

"Yeah?" Henri answered as if Michael's phone call had woken him up.

"Hey, Hen. I have a massive favor to ask."

"Now?"

Henri had never been a morning person, but considering it was nine thirty, Michael thought Henri deserved a kick in the ass for still being in bed. "Well, not right this second, but today."

"Who's that?" Logan's voice was faint enough it didn't sound like he was in bed with Henri. Also, Logan sounded a lot more awake.

"Michael. The fucker," Henri told his boyfriend. Then, into the phone, he asked, "What do you want?"

Michael chewed the inside of his cheek. This was a huge favor, but Henri could be generous if properly motivated.

"I have this friend, and his mom is really sick. Like, well..." Michael didn't know if it was polite to say it with Nicky tucked in his armpit, but there didn't seem to be any other way of putting it. "Like...it's close to the end."

"Oh. Oh, no!" Henri *tsk*ed empathetically, and maybe Michael was shallow for thinking it, but he was glad he'd played to Henri's better nature. "That's so sad."

"Yeah. Well, he has to pack some of her stuff today because she's going to be moving to a nursing home..." Michael wasn't sure that was the right thing to call it, so he added, "Like end-of-life care."

"Wow." Henri blew out a breath. "So tough for him."

"Yeah. Well, the thing is, I offered to help him pack, but I'm supposed to work today." Michael pinched his lips together, waiting for Henri to cotton on to what Michael was asking.

"Wait...who is this guy?"

Michael blinked. It hadn't occurred to him that Henri would ask about Nicky. That seemed immaterial to the question at hand, which was whether Henri would cover for Michael at work. "A friend."

There the words were, floating like a comic book cloud above his head.

"What friend?" The way Henri said it slid right off concerned and into skeptical.

Fuck. Henri may not have liked all of Michael's friends, but he certainly knew most of them well enough that Michael couldn't lie about any of them losing a mother. "A new friend. I..." Shit, the only places Michael went were Speedy Coffee, bars with Jesse and Henri, or to see the guys he knew from school. "It's just a guy I know, okay?"

Michael knew he sounded angry and could not give a damn. Nicky had real problems, not the fake, self-manufactured problems Henri always seemed to come up with. Nicky's were grownup difficulties that no one should have to deal with alone.

Nicky shifted out of his arms, wiping his face as he headed toward the house.

"I'm guessing that you mean *know* in the biblical sense?"

"I'm not going there with you, honey." Michael rarely vamped it up, but talking to Henri always released his inner diva.

"That means yes." Henri was smug.

Fuck it, he could be as smug as he wanted so long as he worked Michael's shift. "Will you go in at eleven? Help Jesse out? I bet I could talk him into closing so long as you help him with the lunch rush." Michael never pleaded, but he did now. Henri would hold it over his head until judgment day.

"Fine. I'll do it. But you *will* tell me about this new boyfriend of yours."

Before Michael could stop himself, he snapped, "He's not my boyfriend."

He wished he hadn't raised his voice, and he wished he hadn't sounded so angry. Michael especially wished Nicky wasn't standing in the window with tears in his eyes.

Chapter Eleven

Nicky shouldn't have been annoyed. Not when Michael had gotten out of work so he could spend the day wrapping Nicky's mom's figurines. Still, Michael saying they weren't boyfriends stung.

"Is it easier for me to come in there, or for you to hand things out?" Michael asked from the hallway.

Nicky had brought a couple of boxes inside, and hurried to put his mother's private things—underwear and nightgowns—in a suitcase before piling her clothes on top. "In a second," Nicky called.

He grabbed anything that seemed too personal for Michael to see and tucked them around her clothes before zipping up the suitcase. "Okay. Yeah. Come in."

Sheepishly, Michael eased in the door. His gaze landed everywhere—on the stuff displayed along her nightstand, on her quilted bedspread, on her window with the shades drawn.

Nicky was glad his mother was napping downstairs because it felt too personal allowing Michael into this space. And yet Nicky needed someone, and he couldn't imagine letting anyone else in.

"You sure she's okay with this?" When Michael spotted the image of Jesus over Nicky's mother's bed, his eyes widened. Anger? Fear? Sadness? Nicky couldn't tell. Maybe he should have warned Michael that his mom's bedroom was even more overwhelming than the living room when it came to the religious stuff. It had never occurred to Nicky why his mother had quite so much paraphernalia around her bed. Now it hit him all in a rush—she'd wanted to be welcomed into heaven if she died in her sleep.

"Hey." Michael stepped up behind him, a hand landing on Nicky's shoulder. "You okay?"

"Yeah." Nicky didn't have the luxury of pondering the configuration of the statues on his mother's dresser. Sick of the stress and the unhappiness that had hung over his head for ages, he grabbed the first of the saints off the nightstand and tossed it to Michael. "Here. Let's get this stuff packed."

"Okay." Michael was silent as he wrapped one after another of Nicky's mother's things, but when Nicky swiped an armful of statues off a surface and dumped them all on the bedspread, Michael raised an eyebrow. "Uh, do you really think she's going to want all this? I mean, how much room will she have?"

Nicky shook his head. He'd seen the space his mom would be afforded at the hospice center. Enough for the cozy chair in the living room, her dresser and nightstand. Part of the entertainment center, though they'd provide her with a TV smaller than the one Nicky had in the living room.

But Nicky refused to do this halfway. He couldn't come home tonight and see things his mom might still want.

"We can sort through it when we get to the center."

Michael was curiously silent as he packed, especially considering he always had an opinion about everything.

"What?" Nicky couldn't keep the anger out of his voice.

"You want me to come with you to drop her off?" Michael's expression was unreadable, though his eyes had darkened.

"Well, no..." Nicky didn't know why he'd assumed Michael would come with him. Maybe in his depression he'd reached for the one delusion that might make this day bearable. Hell, if he really thought about it, Nicky had hoped Michael would drive. With how hard his hands were shaking, Nicky wasn't sure he was safe to be behind the wheel. "I mean, yeah...I can see why you wouldn't want to."

He opened his mom's closet.

Michael came up behind him. "You didn't ask me." There was a testiness in Michael's voice to rival Nicky's own. "I'm not saying I won't come. But...I feel like I'm walking on eggshells. What's the issue?"

The annoyance that had been simmering since Nicky had overheard the phone call boiled over. "I heard what you told your friend."

"Yeah? I told him what I needed to tell him to get him to take my shift at work." Michael reached out, touching Nicky's arm. The way he squeezed and then caressed reminded Nicky so much of his mother and the way she'd always hinted that her love for him was dependent on Nicky towing the line.

He hated that he was thinking bad things about her. Nicky had no right to think ill of his mother. But at that moment, Michael was epitomizing everything wrong in Nicky's world. Michael was going along with the lies Nicky had told all his life, and maybe it made Nicky a hypocrite, but he hated Michael for it. "You told him I was a friend of yours. Like, just some guy you knew."

Michael tugged Nicky to get him to turn. "In case you haven't noticed, we told your mom the same thing last night. And this morning too. I figured that's the story we're telling and I may as well be consistent." Michael lifted his chin.

"That's different and you know it." Nicky scowled, aiming every last bit of his anger at Michael whether he deserved it or not. "You're all out and proud, with your friends and your job where no one cares if you're...the way you are."

"Nice." Michael pursed his lips, his gaze growing more distant by the second. "You can't even say it out loud."

"Like hell I can't." Nicky pushed Michael in the chest. Fuck him, he'd been crowding Nicky anyway. "I'm gay, you're gay. We're clearly together. You slept in my bed last night. And now, what, because I need you, we're suddenly just friends again?"

He wished his anger would stick around, shielding Nicky from what he'd admitted. Maybe Michael hadn't felt anything last night, hadn't felt the shift in the air between them. "Listen, it's too much. You don't have to—"

"Jeez. I wanted to help." Michael tossed his hands in the air. "But God, this is a lot, okay?" There was a crazed look in Michael's eyes, a manic gleam when he ran his hands through his hair. "And I like you, but..."

Nicky wanted to jump in then, cut Michael off before Michael said something scary that Nicky couldn't handle hearing.

"If we're going to be on the down low with some people, I can't be open about what's going on with other people." There was a quick frown on his face, some echo of a thought that Nicky couldn't have guessed.

"Oh." Nicky could imagine it would be easier for Michael to tell everyone the same story. Still, Nicky had wished like hell he could have heard Michael say something that made the two of them seem solid. Maybe not a commitment beyond a casual "yeah, we're seeing each other," but with everything shifting around Nicky like sand, Nicky would have given a lot to have one thing, one connection, that felt permanent. "Yeah, I get that. I guess."

Now he felt like an idiot for getting pissed.

"Are you okay?" Michael's eyes were so blue. Nicky thought the color was called cornflower, though he was pretty sure he'd never actually seen a cornflower in his life. And Michael was helping him even though he didn't have to. God, Nicky could never repay him.

"Yeah." Nicky rubbed his face. He was losing his goddamn mind. "I'm... Well, I shouldn't have gotten pissed. I'm just being..."

Michael landed a hand on Nicky's shoulder. A manly pat and a grip on his skin, but nothing Nicky could read. "You're being like a guy going through something really difficult. I get it, okay?"

Nicky nodded, feeling like a complete douche.

"But I dated a guy once—he was in the closet—and it really messed me up." Michael's eyes begged him to understand. Even through the swirl of ideas going through Nicky's head, Nicky tried to see Michael's point of view. He was risking something too. "Maybe it sounds stupid, but..." Michael shook his head, rubbing a hand along his jaw. "I just need to protect myself."

"Oh." Nicky swallowed against the panic building in his muscles. He turned away so Michael wouldn't see his eyes. "Well, yeah. Okay."

"Don't be like that." Michael touched his arm.

Nicky flinched, throwing him off. "What in the hell do you care?"

"I care because I'm trying to be a friend." Michael's voice rose, but he didn't try to touch Nicky again. In fact, he backed up and started packing. "I think you need one today."

Maybe Michael was right and Nicky was too messed up to be getting serious about any relationship. But fuck, Nicky didn't want to be friends. He wanted Michael to be where he was, feeling the same pain. Really being with Nicky through all of this.

Funny, but a few weeks ago Nicky would have loved a friends with benefits just like Michael, but today he was starting to understand why gay guys felt the need to come out. If no one ever saw that you were a couple, maybe you could never feel like you were.

Kind of like why people got married. They proclaimed their love in front of all the people who mattered to them, and that's what made it real.

"Whatever." Nicky tossed a few knickknacks Michael's direction, though he tried to be more selective about which ones went in the boxes.

"C'mon, Nicky..." Michael stood with a statue of St. Peter in one hand and a garbage bag in the other. "Don't be like that. I really like you. Can't we just...chill for a while? While you sort everything out?"

"Fine." Nicky buried his feelings, trying to be grateful that Michael was doing this much—hanging in there to help when he didn't have to. When the day was over and they'd gotten Nicky's mom off and settled, then Nicky could figure out if he was annoyed enough to tell Michael to take his well-meaning, do-gooder crap and shove it up his ass.

"How about we put the stuff you don't want to take over here for the time being?" Michael moved a pile of books that had been stacked in the corner into the closet next to the shoe rack.

"Fine." Nicky didn't hide the sigh in his voice. If Nicky weren't such a mess, he'd have told Michael to stop bossing him around, but as it was he just handed Michael some spare books and pictures his mom had on her bookshelf.

Michael pulled the Christ painting off the wall. "Take or leave?"

Nicky swallowed, surprised that Michael had lifted the thing off the hook without asking permission. To Nicky, that picture seemed like such a permanent fixture. He'd have thought they'd need a crowbar to pry it loose.

"We should ask about that one." Nicky looked away from the image of Christ's face before he could think on it too hard. "Not sure it'll fit, but I bet my mom wants it."

"You want me to go down?" Michael held it by the wire, backing out of the box-filled room. The hesitance etched between his eyebrows showed he felt as unsettled about things as Nicky was.

"Yeah. That would be great." Nicky kept his eyes on his work. "Thanks." Now that a few of the surfaces were clear of stuff, Nicky had an easier time folding and sorting. He shuffled some of the smaller items into the corner so he could get off his mother's sheets and bedspread.

When he was done, Nicky went to the door, feeling lighter. They were getting there. Finishing the job. Maybe Michael was right and the best thing was for Nicky to power through this and figure out what was between him and Michael later. It had only been a few weeks and a few dates. And Michael liked him. Nicky was overreacting, wanting everything decided between them all at once.

"Hey," he called downstairs, trying to convey with his casual tone that he hoped Michael wasn't mad at him. "Can you grab me some boxes when you come back up?"

There was no answer, so Nicky went into the hallway and then jogged down the stairs. Light poured in the window on the front door, making the house seem brighter than it had in a long time. Things didn't seem so bad. Michael was here, and they were sleeping together. If that wasn't dating, then Nicky didn't know what was.

"So." Nicky rounded into the living room. "What did you decide about the painting?" His eyes had landed on Michael, and Nicky grinned ear to ear to look at the guy. Michael was his friend. With benefits. Nicky was lucky to have that.

"Not sure yet." Michael frowned, his gaze darting to the side.

Nicky panned across the room, his attention landing on Father MacKenzie, who was sitting in his usual armchair.

"Good morning, Nicolas." No one had called Nicky that since he was a kid, and then only when he was in trouble.

"Father." Nicky ducked his head in a quick nod of acknowledgment.

Nicky's mom smiled at Father MacKenzie, a faraway expression on her face, like she was happy to have so many people taking care of her. Too bad there was a squint of suspicion in Father MacKenzie's eyes.

"Aren't you going to introduce me to your *friend*?" Maybe Nicky imagined the way Father MacKenzie seemed to emphasize the word, but Nicky was pretty sure he heard right.

As grateful as he'd been to the priest for coming around to care for his mother, Nicky wished Father MacKenzie could keep his sly glances to himself.

"This is Michael. Michael Larson."

"Nice to meet you, Michael. You and Nicky must be quite close for you to be helping out Nicky like this."

There was no doubt in Nicky's mind that Michael had caught the innuendo. Michael lifted his chin, sticking his nose in the air high enough that Nicky could practically see right up it.

Michael wasn't to blame for wearing a shirt that was too tight or pants that fit his ass like a second skin. Those were Nicky's clothes. But the hand on Michael's hip, his impeccable grooming, heck the way he smirked at the priest in a way that was a direct challenge and more than a little sexual...Michael's gayness was written all over him. He might be willing to lie and claim to be Nicky's *just-a-friend*, but Michael would never, ever lie about being gay. Not to suit Father MacKenzie, not to make Nicky's life easier.

Nicky envied Michael so much right then, maybe even loved him for that bravery. At the same time, Nicky wished Michael didn't have to be so selfish.

"Well, Nicky seemed like he needed all the help he could get." Michael held up the Jesus painting so that Jesus's brown flowing locks were a contrast to Michael's reddish-blond scruff. "So..." He turned his attention to Nicky's mom, his gaze softening instantly. "Do you want us to bring this? Or would you rather keep it here for safekeeping?"

Nicky couldn't have come up with a better, more beautiful way to ask. His mother blinked at the painting, like maybe she didn't even remember it. "Oh, that?" It had been hanging behind her bed for years, and she acted like she'd never seen it before. "Yes, my grandfather brought it over with him when he came to this country. Nicky should keep it here."

Michael lowered the painting, and not sparing a look Father MacKenzie's direction, disappeared past the stairs and into the kitchen.

Nicky readied to follow him, but Father MacKenzie pushed out of his chair. "Nicolas, may I have a word?"

"Yeah, just..." He wished he could follow Michael, say something to tell him it was okay. Fuck, he wished he could go throw himself at Michael's feet and beg him not to leave. No matter what their relationship was or wasn't, he couldn't stand for Michael to storm off angry. But years of Catholic school kicked in, and all Nicky could say was, "Yes, Father."

Nicky went into the front hallway and stared at the floor, waiting for whatever telling off he was going to get.

"Nicky, you know I've been impressed by how well you've been doing here, taking care of your mother like you have."

"I know." Nicky just wanted this over with. Whatever was going to be said, he needed it done with so he could get to Michael before he had time to fume.

"And you know your mother loves you."

Nicky snapped his head up so he could glare at the priest. Whatever Father MacKenzie said about Nicky was fine. He'd cope with it. But if the father said a word, one fucking word, about Nicky's mom, things might come to blows. "And I love her."

"I know you do." The priest must have aimed for a smile, but it came out toothy and wrong. "But just because she's in a weakened state doesn't make it okay to start flaunting your lifestyle."

The words dug in, settled in that place that was raw and open and hurting. His lifestyle. Whatever in the name of God that meant. Nicky was twenty-nine years old and by all reasonable estimations a virgin. He'd never had anyone. Not a girlfriend, not a boyfriend. No one but him and his mom. And now she was leaving him. All he had was this beginning of something with Michael. He was supposed to give it up? Why?

"I have no idea what you're talking about." Nicky wished he had Michael's skill for lifting his nose in the air, answering in a

139

cold, hard voice that told people to go fuck themselves, but all he could do was mumble at the floor like a coward.

Father MacKenzie looked him over, eyes narrowed in suspicion. "Maybe you don't. But I'm sure that boy does."

A car motor sounded outside, and Nicky knew without looking that Michael was leaving. The floor fell out from under him, and if Father MacKenzie was still talking, Nicky didn't hear it. All he understood was the pounding of his heartbeat in his ears as the awareness sank in that Michael was gone.

"Nicky?" Father MacKenzie snapped his fingers like he was trying to get Nicky's attention.

Nicky ignored him, digging in his pocket for his phone. Maybe if he texted...offered to meet Michael somewhere. Maybe Nicky could smooth things over so Michael's pride wasn't quite so injured.

His phone buzzed in his hand.

Ignoring the priest's raised eyebrows, Nicky read the text from Michael.

Heading out to grab some lunch. Will bring you back something. What do you want?

Nicky's eyes filled with tears. He didn't want anything, just for Michael to come back. Michael didn't have to care about him the way Nicky cared about Michael. It was enough that Michael didn't leave for good.

Anything's fine. Whatever you like. Nicky hit send, then couldn't stop himself from adding, *You're awesome. Thanks! I'm so fucking sorry.*

It wasn't what he wanted to type. Shit, Nicky would have said, *I love you.* But if Michael was overwhelmed already my Nicky's neediness, Nicky getting dramatic wasn't going to help.

No worries, Michael replied. *Just tell me when he's gone.*

Nicky knew how much it cost Michael to say that, even as a text message, so he replied right away. *Sure thing.*

"I'm going to say goodbye to your mother. I'll visit once she transitions to All Saints."

Nicky bobbed his head. He hated that things would be on bad terms between him and Father MacKenzie now. The priest wasn't a cruel man. If anything, he was a good person.

"Thanks." Nicky hoped his expression conveyed his gratitude and not the fact that he could have punched Father MacKenzie in the face.

By the time Michael and Nicky had loaded the boxes in the cavernous trunk of the Town Car, the hottest part of the day had passed, and Michael had all but shucked off his annoyance over the priest encounter.

I'm doing this for Nicky... Being a friend...

That had been his mantra all day, especially when he'd pulled out of Nicky's driveway fully intending to head back to the University District. A boyfriend? No, he couldn't be that. Michael would *never* put up with the looks that priest had given him. Not even for a guy he cared about.

Nicky led his mom in wobbling footsteps down her front stairs. Michael should have looked away. He'd learned in his short time with Lydia that she didn't like Michael noticing how sick she was. She'd frown when she coughed in his presence, and always waited until he was out of the room to ask Nicky for help.

Nicky opened the passenger-side door and offered it to his mother, but she shook her head.

Maybe her priest had warned her off him, Satan spawn that he was. Michael fiddled with the volume on the radio, trying to distract himself from the thought. Lydia had been perfectly nice to him, polite, welcoming.

Of course, she might have acted differently if she knew he was gay, but... He glanced in the rearview mirror and saw her face in the backseat. The pain crinkling the edges of her eyes. Cheeks so hollowed out they seemed blue. Maybe she was homophobic and maybe she wasn't, but Michael would never find out the answer. Not unless Nicky decided to come clean with her. And honestly, Michael didn't even know if he wanted Nicky to.

"You ready?" Nicky slipped into the passenger seat. His smile was more like two lips pinched together and his eyes resigned.

"Yeah. Mapped it out on GPS and everything." Michael started the tedious process of backing the monster sedan out of the driveway. A couple hours after the worst of the traffic, he still had to wait a minute before he could coast, like a ship set free of its moorings, backwards into the road.

"Thanks for driving." Nicky sighed. He looked over his shoulder, which caused Michael to glance in the rearview again.

Nicky's mom had tears in her eyes. She wasn't wiping them away, either, just letting them roll down her cheeks to pool on her upper lip.

Michael was glad he was driving, so he had an excuse not to watch.

"I remember when your father bought this car for me." Her voice quivered and was full of phlegm and feeling. "He was so excited."

Nicky's chuckle was watery, but Michael couldn't bear to look his direction to find out if Nicky was crying as freely as his mother. Michael couldn't afford to give in to emotion along with them. He needed his vision clear to drive.

"Yeah, remember how we went to Olympia that day, just because it had air conditioning?"

Nicky and his mother went back and forth like that, reminiscences and stories that let Michael think his own thoughts about how the last twenty-four hours had been some of the most intense in his life. Maybe the most intense. And how he'd resolved not to tell anyone he and Nicky were dating.

The hospice center was twenty minutes from Nicky's house, located on a bluff surrounded by evergreens. It wasn't close to any businesses, only some warehouses spaces, which must have made the location affordable.

They took Nicky's mom inside, Michael feeling more like a third wheel than ever while Nicky filled out all the paperwork. The staff took Lydia to her room, and Michael busied himself carrying boxes and unpacking things that a few hours ago he'd bundled up safely.

"You've been so nice to help Nicky out with all this," Lydia said to him from her bed where the staff was fussing to make sure it was at an angle to her liking and the right distance from the TV.

"Um...thanks." Since the showdown with Lydia's priest friend, Michael had been trying to say as little to her as possible. Part of him worried that at any moment she'd ask him if he was gay and fucking her son.

But although one of the nursing staff—a guy who was in fact clearly gay—gave Michael a half smile, Lydia continued as if nothing was amiss between him and Nicky. "He's worked so hard. And I know it's not easy. A boy his age. Maybe he can go out sometimes now that he doesn't have to be home so much. You could introduce him to some girls."

The gay nurse, or nurse's aide, or whatever his position was, snorted lightly, and Michael hoped like hell that Lydia hadn't noticed.

"Yeah. I'll make sure he has some fun." He met her eyes. They'd dried since the car, maybe a side effect of the aggressively cheery surroundings. The walls were pale yellow, soothing and light like a sunrise, with wallpaper trim that managed to look homey without being completely kitsch.

One of the aides, not the gay one, got to work arranging and unpacking Lydia's stuff, and Michael hated to admit it, but he was relieved.

"Hey." Nicky ducked his head in. "Can I talk to you for a sec?"

"Sure." Michael slipped out of the room and into a hallway that was robin's-egg blue. As pleasant as the color was, it didn't quite cover that the place smelled like a hospital.

"Listen." Nicky spoke in low tones, his face half hidden by hair, which as far as Michael could tell he hadn't cut since Michael had first met him. "Um…it's only family and a short list of friends who are allowed in my mom's room. I could ask her to add you, but she's had so much going on today…"

Michael let out a long breath through his nose, trying to shuck off his annoyance. He'd spent the whole damn day helping Nicky pack, called in sick to work, which he'd never done in his life. Now Michael was getting shoved out the door like last week's garbage. *Nice.* "It's fine."

The gay aide chose that moment to pass by, smirking and giving Nicky an appraising once-over.

Michael glowered at the guy. For fuck's sake, Nicky was moving his mom into hospice care. What kind of asshole would be cruising Nicky at a time like this?

"I'm gonna say good night to my mom." Nicky wiped his nose. He went into his mom's room, leaving Michael in the hallway. Though Nicky was only gone a few minutes, it was long enough for Michael's annoyance to dig deeper, getting under his skin and into his bones. When Nicky finally came out of the room, Michael found he didn't have any words of comfort to offer.

"You want to go?"

Michael nodded. "Sure." He followed Nicky outside to where the sun was starting to set. As much as Michael knew he should take Nicky's hand, or rub his arm, or even give him a kiss, once they were driving Michael couldn't bring himself to reach across the armrest.

"Are you going to stay over again tonight?" Nicky stared out the window, the random passes of streetlights flashing over his pale skin.

"I don't know if that's a good idea." Michael held his breath. It wasn't that Michael was mad, so much, or even hurt, but he needed space. Or maybe time. He needed to get back in control and to a place where he didn't feel like he was being dragged over hot coals. "I mean, I can if you want, but maybe it's best if I stay on the couch."

Michael could do that much. Be a friend to Nicky tonight, since that was what Nicky probably needed. Just a steady presence so he wouldn't be alone.

"Yeah, right," Nicky scoffed, his gaze focused on something out the window. "Maybe you should go home instead then."

Michael pulled into Nicky's driveway, having parked his rental car on the street. The night was cool, blowing in the upper edge of the Town Car's windows. Nicky sat shadowed in the front seat like that night in Seward Park, but so different it might have happened last century instead of a few weeks ago.

"Nicky…" Michael tried to get control of his temper, when all he wanted to do was lash out. "I'm not going to leave if you're upset." Neither was he going to let Nicky treat him like shit, but Michael stuffed those words deep so he wouldn't say them out loud. "I get that you may need—"

"And what about what you need?" Nicky nailed Michael with a glare.

Michael shrank in his seat, taken back by Nicky's anger. Annoyed that Nicky was suddenly and inexplicable turning the tables when Nicky had never once in all of this asked what Michael wanted. "I don't know what you're talking about." He heard his voice rising and wished he could keep it under control. "I'm fine. The day was a little intense, but—"

"Jesus. Forget I said anything." Nicky opened his door, letting air rush into the musty space. He moved to climb out, but Michael caught his arm.

"For fuck's sake. Don't be angry."

Nicky yanked his arm away. "Don't tell me what to feel."

"I'm not." Michael rubbed his face. A headache throbbed at the base of his skull, and after the day they'd had, he couldn't unscramble his thoughts well enough to be eloquent. "I'm just trying to be your friend."

Nicky's glare could have melted paint off walls. "I don't want you to be my friend, asshole. I never did." With a slam of the door, Nicky stormed toward the door of his house.

Michael watched him go, unsure whether to follow or to drive home. Nicky turned on lights in the hallway, and then the living room. And Michael could have sworn he heard something crash inside.

He got out of the Lincoln to head back to his own car. The air had cooled enough to be chilly, and Michael rubbed his arms under his borrowed shirt sleeves. Michael's clothes were still at Nicky's place. Hell, his messenger bag, computer and toothbrush were in there too.

Michael had to go back, but he could more easily imagine walking into a den of lions. What did Nicky want from him? Michael had done everything right. He'd been the good guy— unlike the letch at the nursing home or the priest who'd stared Michael down like he was a piece of shit on the sidewalk.

Michael was in the right. So why was he standing outside in the dark, listening for the next thing Nicky would break, or waiting for Nicky to come outside and scream away on his motorcycle on some death ride?

His phone vibrated in his pocket, and Michael groaned to see Henri's name flashing on his screen. Michael wouldn't have answered it except he'd mortgaged Henri's goodwill for a day off. A lot of good it had done. Nicky seemed even more upset now than he had that morning.

"Well, hello, man of mystery." Henri's voice was jovial. He was probably out at some bar with Logan.

"Hey, Hen. Listen, thanks. You really helped me out earlier. Seriously." He couldn't begin to explain, and Michael was pretty sure he didn't want to try. "But I can't talk right now." Michael watched as Nicky turned on what seemed like every light in the house. What was Nicky doing? Crying? Drinking? Nicky shouldn't have been Michael's responsibility, but somehow in the last twenty-four hours, it felt like he was.

The house drew Michael like a magnet, and he wondered what lay inside. Shouting, maybe? Angry looks? Down to the very marrow, Michael knew what else was waiting...a real relationship.

Maybe that was the reason Michael didn't want to go in there. He couldn't make love to Nicky like they were soul mates and act like they were just friends in the morning.

"Okay." Henri had a funny tenor in his voice. "I won't keep you, but I have to ask—and this is only because I care that I'm asking this—is this friend you're helping out Mark?"

"No. It's not Mark. And we broke up four fucking years ago, in case you forgot. I haven't even spoken to the guy since—"

"Okay. Okay. It's just...well, I know most of the guys you're friends with."

Michael slid into the passenger side of his rental car. He'd forgotten his casserole dish at Nicky's as well, and the racking up of reasons to go up those steps and knock on Nicky's door was beating Michael into submission.

He pushed the key into the ignition and turned on the electricity so he could get some heat. Compared to Nicky's mom's car, the Mazda felt empty. Not simply of knickknacks and scuffs and all the things that made a car lived-in, but emotions as well. The car was a shell. Useful, nothing more. "He's just someone I know, okay? I am allowed to have other friends."

"Don't pretend you're not sleeping with this guy."

Michael closed his eyes and leaned against the headrest. Fucking Henri. "No. I'm not sleeping with him." *Not technically, at least.*

"Well, in that case it's worse because it means that you want to and can't."

Henri's words rang in Michael's head. Because Michael didn't only want to sleep with Nicky, he wanted to do everything with Nicky. Be everything for Nicky. He wanted to run right back to that fucking house and gather Nicky up in his arms.

He wanted to rescue Nicky from himself and from his fears and even from other gay men who might take advantage of Nicky's weakened and suggestible state. If he was being honest, Michael wanted to let go and love the guy. Give in to all that

148

need he saw in Nicky's eyes and let Nicky think Michael was his everything.

"I could sleep with him if I wanted to." Not that it mattered.

"Oh, honey..."

Michael knew from Henri's tone that his friend was going to launch into a round of unsolicited advice. Right, because finally managing a relationship that wasn't totally abusive made Henri an authority on dating.

"I should go." Michael rubbed his legs, warming up in the heat of the vents from the car. There was no use putting it off. He had to go back into Nicky's house. But he had no idea what he'd do when he got there. "Listen, I'll call you tomorrow, okay."

"You'll really call me?" Henri's voice was stern over the hum of techno music in the background on his end.

Not about Nicky. "Sure." Michael rubbed a hand over the logo on his shirt, a reminder that he'd drifted so far out of his comfort zone that he wasn't even wearing his own clothes. "I'll call you tomorrow."

Chapter Twelve

Nicky paced the living room. He'd gotten the hospital bed apart, but most of the space was the same as it had been for weeks, months, maybe years. Same darkness. Same musty smell. The dent in the center of the couch where his mom had always sat made it look like she was only in the bathroom and would wander back any moment.

Worse than that, Michael still being outside was like itching powder under Nicky's skin. He picked up the remote and turned on the giant TV set to have noise to counteract the silence.

Staring, he tried to make sense of what was on the screen. Something involving cops and crime. Without his mother to watch with, the bright flickering set seemed obscene. No light should glow when his mother was gone. Not even some stupid show he'd watched with her a thousand times.

Fitfully, he shut off the set. Then Nicky folded a random box into the right shape and tossed it on the floor. He needed to get rid of some of this stuff—now.

Maybe Michael was leaving and maybe he wasn't. Nicky had to stop giving a shit. Michael didn't care. Not like Nicky did. Michael's heart wasn't wrapped in leather and getting tighter by the second.

Nicky threw a box at the corner.

Fucking do-gooder Mr. Nice Guy. Michael didn't even realize how much he was being an ass.

Grabbing a lamp, Nicky ripped off the shade. He hated the damn thing, and now that his mother wasn't around to argue against getting rid of it, he'd finally toss it in the trash.

"Fuck!" The carved wood of the lamp dug a splinter into Nicky's palm. He winced, squeezing his eyes tight. He wouldn't let a tear escape. Not another one, and not when Michael might come back in any second and see. Nicky could be hard and cold too. Lift his fucking nose in the air and act like he was better than everybody.

Storming into the kitchen, he fumbled through cabinets for a Band-Aid. Sitting on the counter was Michael's casserole dish. Nicky wanted to throw the damn thing across the room. Hell, he wanted to smash half the house to pieces.

He grabbed a beer out of the fridge, and even though he and Michael hadn't eaten dinner, he downed the entire thing.

As he opened his second beer, he wondered if Michael had left yet. Part of him wanted to call and find out. The rest of him wanted to hear a screech of tires that meant Michael was gone.

A knock from the front door sounded through the house. Slowly and very deliberately Nicky set his beer on the counter. He wouldn't cry. Michael didn't deserve the satisfaction. Tipping his chin up, Nicky made his way to the door. When he opened it, Nicky pressed his lips together so he'd neither frown nor smile.

"Hey." Michael stood tall and straight as a rod, his hands fisting and unfisting as if he was trying to act calmer than he was. "Um, I realized I left my clothes here. And my laptop."

Nicky should have slammed the door in Michael's face. Or told him to wait outside and thrown his shit at him. But Nicky wouldn't give Michael another ounce of feeling. "Fine." Crossing

151

his arms, Nicky stepped to the side to let Michael pass. "Grab your stuff."

"Oh. Come on, Nicky." Michael tossed up his hands. "I don't get why you're mad at me."

"I'm not mad." Inside Nicky was fuming, but no way would he let Michael see it. "If you want your stuff, come in and get it."

Michael's face twisted into an expression that was concern mixed with something else. Regret?

It better as hell not be pity.

"Fine." Michael pushed past Nicky and headed to the kitchen. "I'll get out of your way then."

For once, Michael's gait had a jerkiness to it, like he was lifting his feet too high in an effort to march rather than walk. He grabbed the casserole dish first, but tripped on the steps on the way up and fumbled the plate before catching it on a stair.

"Fuck," he mumbled, though Michael kept his trek up to Nicky's room.

Nicky waited downstairs, expecting for Michael to return right away. Instead, Michael seemed to take a long time gathering things. Step by step, Nicky eased his way up the stairs. At the top landing, his door was open.

Michael was in that room. Crying? Scowling? Frowning? Nicky wished he could force himself not to look and not to care. Maybe there would be nothing but Michael's cool exterior when Nicky went in there, but he had to find out. If there was pain on Michael's face, Nicky had to see it, just to know if Michael could bleed too.

Nicky peered inside to find Michael shirtless. He had tossed Nicky's shirt in the laundry pile and was holding his own stretched between his arms like he was about to put it on.

His eyes were shadowed, sad. Hesitant in a way Nicky was pretty sure he'd never seen before.

Michael shrugged. "I thought you'd want your clothes back," he said by way of explanation.

"Right." Nicky stormed into the room to slap Michael's laptop shut. "Because God forbid I'd have to go to your place to pick stuff up."

"I don't get it." Michael dropped his arms so the shirt fell away from his body and was scrunched between his twisting hands.

"You don't get what?"

"I don't get what you want from me." Michael's eyes had never been bluer. Gone was his upright, squared-shoulder posture. He dipped his head like he could find the answer in Nicky's eyes. "I can't do this." For maybe the first time since they met, Michael seemed vulnerable. Like someone Nicky might actually be able to hurt. "Not if I can't tell other people. I just can't."

"Jesus!" Nicky snatched the shirt out of Michael's hands and tossed it by the laundry. Maybe it was a stupid gesture, but Michael was not leaving. At least not until Nicky had said his piece. "Could you give me a few weeks at least? Maybe a day or two after I just packed my mother's things and took her to a hospice center?" Nicky advanced a step, wanting to shove Michael but knowing instinctively that if things between them got physical, he'd be saying goodbye to Michael forever. Michael wasn't the type of guy to push and wrestle in anger. He'd never forgive it if Nicky truly lost his temper.

"Like I don't know that. I've been here all day. Going through all of it with you."

Nicky dropped his gaze. No Michael hadn't. Not really. Michael always kept things at arm's length. Under control. "Oh right. I forgot. Being my *friend*."

Michael stayed stonily silent for so long that Nicky eventually dragged back his gaze. Shirtless, Michael seemed paler than normal. He only had a little hair on his chest, and his nipples were a rosy shade of pink. Funny, Nicky had never actually seen Michael bare before. Not with the lights on.

"I get that you need time." Michael crossed his arms, as if maybe he needed to cover up in Nicky's presence. "But maybe I do too. Have you thought about that?"

Truth was, Nicky did understand. At least his brain did. But his heart was so tied up in knots, he couldn't quite connect what he felt with what he thought.

"Whatever." He wished he hadn't sounded so mean. He hadn't meant to. Fuck, Michael was the one person he most cared about after his mom. But Nicky couldn't be angry with her. Not for choosing hospice care, not for all the religious imagery in the house that made him feel like there was no way he could come clean about who he was.

He couldn't be mad at her for anything, so he threw it—like a flying tornado of fury—at Michael. "Take all the time you need."

"Oh, will you stop it with the martyr routine?" Michael marched past Nicky to where his laptop sat next to his messenger bag. He shoved it inside.

As much as Nicky wanted to tell him *fuck you* and *leave, why don't you*, panic welled up inside him at the thought that Michael might really do it.

"Stop."

Michael paused, hand on his bag's clasp, face impassive. He waited. Nicky knew there was something he could say to make Michael not leave. But fuck if Nicky knew what it was.

"Have sex with me." The words were out before Nicky knew he'd said them. They sounded weird, and yet totally right. As much as Nicky was angry and confused, he needed to escape. He wanted to feel a pain besides the dead weight in his gut. Michael could transport him from this place. Hell, he could drag Nicky right out of his head until Nicky didn't care about anything but coming in Michael's arms.

"Nicky, I don't think that's what you need tonight." Michael's body was still, his voice a flat tenor.

Nicky could tell Michael wanted it. Even if Michael wouldn't admit it to himself.

"Why don't you let me worry about what I need?" Nicky took a slow step forward, then another. He dragged his shirt over his head, knowing that it would tempt Michael into action. "I have to feel something else tonight. Not sad..." Nicky put his fingertips on Michael's arm. There was a tan line right above Michael's biceps. Touching the paler, smoother skin felt like reaching a place he never had. "And I don't want to feel overwhelmed anymore."

Michael trembled under Nicky's touch. The muscles on his lean frame were taut and flat, like a runner's. His shoulders rolled forward like one push and he'd sprint away.

"I wanna get fucked," Nicky admitted for the first time in his life. "And I think you want to fuck me. And it doesn't have to mean anything." In Nicky's mind, it would mean everything. Be everything. But he couldn't push Michael any further tonight. Maybe Michael would take off in the morning. In fact, he might take off right after. But if that happened, at least Nicky would have something of him.

"Like fuck it doesn't have to mean anything." The way Michael murmured was angry, but Nicky knew Michael was going to give in.

"Really." Nicky unfastened his belt and then the button fly of his jeans. He stripped naked right there, with Michael's attention still on his messenger bag.

When Nicky was naked, he stood like an offering. The cool night air chilled him, raising goose bumps on his shoulders and arms and legs. He waited for Michael to turn and see him, to acknowledge everything Nicky was willing to give.

"Why are you doing this?" Michael rolled his gaze down Nicky's body before dropping it once again to the bedspread.

"Because you won't." Nicky rotated Michael so they were pressed together. Though Nicky had been mostly soft with anxiety up until now, the feel of Michael, long and sinewy against him, had him filling with need.

He reached for Michael's ass. Pulled him close so they ground together.

"I want it." He pushed his hips against Michael's and wrapped his arms around Michael's neck. He could feel the reluctance in Michael's tense muscles.

"Come on." Nicky rubbed Michael's back, up warm ridges and bone. "It's okay. Just take it."

For a long moment, they stood there, entwined but barely moving. Nicky could practically hear Michael's brain going a mile a minute, coming up with ways to justify or validate or otherwise intellectualize what they were about to do.

Nicky could have grabbed Michael's dick and urged things along, but Nicky didn't want to. He needed Michael to be the one to make the next move, the next decision. Nicky refused to be in this alone. If he was sacrificing his body at the altar of their fledgling relationship, the least Michael could do was accept his gift with enthusiasm.

"Okay." Michael cupped Nicky's jaw. For the first time since the doorway, his eyes met Nicky's. They'd gone gray with emotion. "Okay, Nicky," he whispered. "I will."

As Michael leaned in to kiss him, he tried to silence the bleating voice in his head that screamed *run*. Feelings this intense weren't real. They were like mushrooms or ecstasy, artificial and fleeting and left you wrung out and empty afterwards.

Michael had never been interested in drugs. Not even freshman year in college when it seemed most people were stoned constantly. No, his drug of choice back then had been Mark. His closeted, uncaring ex who always left Michael feeling so high he never wanted to come down.

There'd been no safety net, no agreement between him and Mark for Michael to hold on to, and maybe that was what made it so exciting. Now, hope for a relationship dangled just out of reach. That was almost worse than not having it at all. Because what if Michael really did fall? He'd expect Nicky to catch him, and maybe—like Mark had done again and again—Nicky would pull away when Michael needed him most.

Nicky's mouth opened under Michael's, and their tongues tangled. Michael kissed like he could take that control back, like he could pull in the reins on his feelings until Nicky was the one panting and Michael didn't feel any longer like the world had slipped from under his feet.

In a quick shuffle, Michael dragged his clothes off. He couldn't touch Nicky enough. The scruff of hair on Nicky's chest, leading in a thin trail down his stomach. The cock jutting forward, batting against Michael's. He pushed Nicky to get him on his back on the bed, and before Michael could get swept away, he climbed on top.

He thrust into Nicky's hip, savoring the sensation of them together. In four years, Michael hadn't gotten his heart involved when he had sex with a guy. Now his ribs felt too tight, like they couldn't contain everything he wanted to give.

"But slow, okay?" Michael couldn't handle fast. The sex would burn too bright, leave him hung over and empty.

"Yeah." Nicky wrapped his legs around Michael's back. Their cocks rubbed together, already familiar and yet deliciously new.

"God." Michael ran his palm down Nicky's back and grabbed a handful of meaty rear. He might have felt like his soul was being ripped out of his body, but he could still appreciate the very physical sensation of heat and power in his palm. "You have the greatest ass."

Nicky's leg hair was sparse and ended with a little tuft right behind his balls. So different from the waxed-and-groomed guys Michael knew from school and from clubs. Maybe it was his mom's hippie influence, but Michael had always liked hair on a guy. It held their smell and tickled Michael's skin.

Michael teased Nicky's crease with slow passes of his fingertips. "You like this?" He eased them onto their sides, facing each other, so he could watch the emotions play out on Nicky's face.

"Oh God." Nicky twisted to bury his face in the pillow.

"No." Michael touched his jaw. "Want you to look at me."

Slowly, Nicky turned his head.

"Wanna see you when I get you open." Michael rolled up to get supplies out of his messenger bag, flicking off the light in the process. When the room was dim, with only light filtering around the crack in the door, Michael eased back so he and Nicky faced each other.

"Now, where were we?" Michael poured some lube on his hand, taking longer than necessary so he could watch nerves battle with excitement on Nicky's face.

"Um?"

Reaching around Nicky's hip, Michael wiped the lube into Nicky's crease. He teased and pressed, getting closer and closer to Nicky's opening. "Lift your leg."

Nicky whimpered, but cocked his knee up to widen his thighs.

Michael eased closer to kiss him gently, then reached between his legs. With a single fingertip, he pushed inside. Nicky clamped down immediately and humped at Michael's forearm like he'd come in a second.

"Hey." Michael swatted Nicky's rump. "Slow down." Now that they were this far, Michael didn't want Nicky shooting before Michael was buried inside him. Michael needed that closeness.

"Okay." Nicky's forehead crumpled and he bit his lip—all the encouragement Michael needed to keep pushing.

"Now, I want you to stay loose this time. Let me all the way in."

Though Nicky nodded like crazy, Michael doubted he'd be able to follow directions. Michael gathered a little more lubricant on his fingers and rubbed it around Nicky's hole before slowly pressing inside.

To his surprise, Nicky's passage stayed soft. Tight, but not the clenched-muscle tightness from before. Michael watched Nicky's face, how his mouth was slack and his eyes kept drifting closed. Michael worked one finger all the way in.

An anguished grunt broke from Nicky's mouth.

"You like?" Michael pulled out so he could start the process of getting in a second finger. "Want my cock up there?"

The moment his two fingertips pressed past Nicky's muscles, Nicky clenched. Face tense, he pumped his hips like he could fuck through Michael's skin.

"Hey." Michael smacked Nicky's ass harder this time, right over the spot that was still warm from his last blow. "I told you—relax."

"Oh God." Nicky rubbed his forehead in the pillow. His cheeks were bright pink, and he was about the most gorgeous man Michael had ever seen.

Michael tried to stay distanced, detached. He knew it was a losing fight. "Can you do it for me?" Michael worked both fingers deep into Nicky's crease. "Soft, soft, soft..."

Nicky blew out a long breath, his body slick and tempting around Michael's fingers, his shoulders slumping on the bed.

"That's it." Feeling the give in the muscles, Michael worked Nicky open. Stroking and rubbing, pulling out before pushing back inside to the knuckle. Though Nicky whimpered the whole time, he didn't make a move to tense or thrust. "That's so good," Michael cooed. Most guys took ages to give in as much as Nicky was. Michael had heard way too many horror stories of guys getting hurt because they moved too fast.

"Look at me." He understood that Nicky might be too worked up to talk, but Michael needed to make sure he wasn't in pain.

When Nicky lifted his head to face Michael, everything Nicky was feeling was written all over his features. He was flushed, pupils blown wide, lips damp and parted.

Michael kissed him, tasting his breath.

"You okay?" Michael asked against his mouth. "Because I'm almost ready to fuck you."

"Oh God. Oh fuck. Oh God..." Nicky's jaw tensed.

"Here we go." Michael turned them over, getting between Nicky's legs. He tucked a pillow under Nicky's hips so his knees rose between his shoulders. "Same rules. Stay loose or I'll stop."

Nicky nodded, gulping like he couldn't get enough air.

"Just relax." Michael grabbed a condom and rolled it down in a quick swipe. Then he positioned his tip against the folded skin of Nicky's hole.

"Don't clench." Michael eased his cap into Nicky's opening, watching for signs that it was too much. When he got in an inch, Nicky started to shake.

"Oh God." Nicky's glutes clamped around him.

Michael didn't hesitate before landing a smack across his ass. "Hey. What did I tell you?" He knew the place Nicky was in, how Nicky needed to be told and pushed and even maybe forced a little. Michael remembered from back when he'd been with Mark. He'd been so cranked up on endorphins he'd thought Mark was a god. Michael wanted to give Nicky that excitement. He wanted Nicky to feel that way about him so that maybe Nicky would be too attached to ever push Michael away.

"I didn't mean. Just... Don't stop." Nicky grabbed behind his knees to tip his ass up, damp with sweat and lube, and tempting as anything.

Michael gripped an ass cheek, cracking Nicky wide and getting his dick in place again. He used gentle pressure, slow invasions pulling those delicate folds taut. When he felt the resistance of Nicky's muscles, Michael paused. "Just a little more, Nicky. You can take it, okay? It'll hurt some, but you'll like it so much."

Nicky nodded.

"Don't tense." Michael knew his words were in vain, because when he pressed inward, Nicky clamped down hard. With Michael already past his rings of muscle, all his clenching did was drag Michael deeper inside.

"Fuuuuuck... So good." Michael climbed farther on top to rest his weight on Nicky's chest.

Nicky's whole body vibrated. "Oh God..."

Michael stroked down Nicky's side. "That's it. Try and relax. Let it feel good."

"Can't..." Nicky gasped. "Gotta come. Gotta..."

Michael's heart could have cracked open, that was how close he felt to Nicky right then. He wanted Nicky to feel everything. To have everything. It was totally different from how it had been with Mark, because then Michael had been the one giving and Mark had just taken.

"So good." Michael kissed him right behind his ear, where his stubble had grown in. He tasted like sweat. "Just a little longer, okay?"

Everything in Nicky's heart leapt to his throat—his emotions, his sadness, even the anger and regret that came in waves he couldn't control some days. All of it was okay because Michael was inside him. Because Michael made everything bearable.

Michael arched his hips, pushing his thrusts farther, farther. The sting washed over Nicky, spreading from his hole through his dick and belly.

When Nicky finally gave in to the screaming-sinew need to tighten his muscles, Michael gasped like Nicky had ripped him in half.

"Fuck." Michael pumped a short thrust.

Nicky couldn't tell if it was because he was trying to be gentle or because Nicky had him caught tightly enough he couldn't move. "I can't..." Nicky tried to breathe, he tried to do anything, because nothing on the planet could have unwound him enough to relax at that moment. His orgasm curled in his balls, twisting through the pain and dragging Nicky higher than he'd ever been before. Michael had better move faster soon, or this was all going to be over.

"Don't move." Michael wiggled his hips, rolling in short thrusts more like vibration than strokes.

"I...I just can't..." Nicky mouthed curses. He could tell from Michael's panted whines that Michael was close too, but God, Nicky hoped he wasn't hurting the guy.

"There. That's better."

Nicky must have loosened a fraction because Michael had more movement now, grinding in tight circles. Michael changed his angle, and he nailed the right spot in a nonstop twist and curl.

"Fucking hell..." Nicky pushed a hand between them to grip his cock and found that with every shove of Michael's hips, Nicky's dick was forced through the cuff of his fingers. Fuck, if he only had...

"Here." Michael pushed a lube bottle at Nicky's shoulder.

Nicky would have gasped out a joke about Michael's preparedness, but his brain had turned to Jell-O and his body to molten lava. Messily, he got a dollop on his hand, and while he tried to get his fist between them, Michael pulled out, dripped some more lube into Nicky's crease, and then pushed back in with an excruciating slowness that had Nicky moaning.

"Yes. Fuck, Nicky. That's it."

Now Nicky knew what Michael meant about being open. He couldn't quite manage to do it on purpose, but he felt the slip and the slide, the give that let Michael's thrusts go all the way to his center. Letting Michael in. That's what he'd meant to do all along.

Michael slammed into him, his aim messier, and each thrust pushed Nicky through his palm full of lube and another few inches up the bed. "Yeah, Nicky. God..." Michael sounded like he was crying. His body tensed, but his hips snapped a slow, deep beat Nicky couldn't help but feel the echo of until Nicky was coming right along with Michael. A spasm, a thrust, another spasm that started in Nicky's ass but spread through his cock and his balls until his hand was sticky.

"God." Michael dropped on top of him, sweaty and slick and mashing come between them.

Nicky buried his face in Michael's neck. He didn't know if anything had been decided, or whether they were a couple now or not. But Nicky was forever changed. He hoped like hell that Michael felt the same.

Michael shifted, pulling out in the process. He flopped onto his back. "Okay, I don't mean to be a freak, but we should shower."

"You're not a freak." Nicky didn't push for anything. It would only lead back to a road he didn't want to travel. Anyway, his ass couldn't take another round of distracting Michael from leaving. Nicky landed a kiss on Michael's lips and started getting out of bed. He was sore in odd places and wanted a chance to clean up on his own, rather than having Michael come at him with a pile of towelettes. "Can I get the bathroom first?"

"Yeah. Sure." Michael's voice was breathy and maybe a little nervous. Nicky wished it were darker so he didn't see the worry on Michael's face.

"I'll see ya in a sec." Nicky made his way to the door, grabbing a shirt so he wouldn't be walking through the house naked.

"Yeah." There was reluctance in Michael's voice. "Um...do you want me to take the couch downstairs, then? Or the bed in your mom's room? You should really sleep in the bed tonight, hon."

Nicky's chest swelled with feeling, but he wouldn't call Michael out on his chivalry. He knew Michael would only balk and claim he was sleeping over because it was what Nicky needed.

"Whichever you want." Nicky couldn't think too hard on the weirdness of Michael sleeping in places his mom had been recently. "There are fresh sheets above the washing machine in the hall."

Chapter Thirteen

"So, uh...do you want to do something tonight?" Michael set his coffee cup on the kitchen table and turned away to look in the cabinet for cereal. He and Nicky had been distant and formal all morning, but with Michael heading to work in an hour, Michael hoped to come up with a plan for the next time they'd meet.

In particular, he wanted to start steering their relationship in the "out" direction. Because there was no denying it. They were dating. And Michael would drag Nicky out of the closet kicking and screaming if necessary.

Nicky picked up Michael's cup and took a sip out of it before opening the fridge to bend inside. "Sure. Like a movie?"

After the fireworks of their time together the night before, Michael wasn't surprised Nicky was a little on edge.

"I was thinking maybe a bar. With some friends of mine." Michael tensed, hoping Nicky didn't balk and ruin Michael's bubble of expectation.

"Yeah. I guess." Nicky pulled some milk out of the fridge, his eyes guarded. He looked about twelve in his baggy sleep shirt and shorts. "You'd let me meet your friends?"

"Yeah. Of course." Michael took a chance and reached for Nicky's waist. Nicky came into his arms easily. More easily than

Michael would have expected considering they both seemed to be treading carefully. "Why wouldn't I?"

"I don't know." Nicky shrugged. "Do you need me to invite you to do something with the guys I know after? To be honest, I don't know if I'm up for that yet."

For an instant, Michael's hands tightened in annoyance, but he tried to shake out the feeling before Nicky could react. This didn't all have to happen in a day. Nicky had said a lot of things that had pissed Michael off the night before, but Nicky had been right about one thing—coming out didn't have to occur in one fell swoop, or in a grand gesture where Nicky gathered up and told everyone he knew all at once.

Meeting Michael's friends was a step. One of many. The first had been when Nicky invited him to dinner.

"It's okay." Michael tried to believe it was true, and he mostly did. "Though a couple of my friends are dating firefighters. Not sure you know them, but..." Michael had no idea how fast word might get around. He may as well lay out the situation for Nicky.

Nicky pulled in a breath deep enough to make his chest expand. He held it, like he wasn't sure what to do, then blew it out in an exhalation that made him look like he'd shrunk two sizes. "That's fine. I mean... It's not like it's some big secret."

Michael twisted to grab more coffee, mostly to hide his smile.

"But would it be, like, a gay bar?"

"I don't know." Michael hadn't set up anything concrete yet. He certainly wasn't going to take Nicky anywhere too edgy. "I mean, there'd be gay people there, I guess." Most of the places Michael and his friends went were a mixed bag of straights, gays and hipsters of questionable orientation. But he supposed the bar may be more gay than Nicky was used to.

167

"Do I need to wear anything specific?"

Michael was pretty sure Nicky didn't own anything besides Levi's and sweatpants. "It's not like we'd go to a club or anything." As brave of a face as Nicky put on, Michael knew asking the guy to dance was out of the question. "Your normal clothes'll be fine." When Nicky's forehead creased like he was worried, Michael laughed. "I'll help you dress later, okay?"

"Yeah. Sure." Nicky cracked a small smile. "After I visit my mom, though, okay?"

"Of course." Michael put his hand on Nicky's arm. No way would Michael expect Nicky to suddenly abandon his mother now that she wasn't living in his house. Though Michael did think Nicky could stand a little more time to have fun.

In fact, Michael had promised Nicky's mother he'd help Nicky have fun. Though it was weird and twisted, and maybe he was misinterpreting the edict, Michael planned to do as she'd said. "Yeah. Visit your mom. I'll see you when I get home from work."

The place Michael's friends had named turned out to be a cleaner and slightly brighter version of the types of places Nicky's friends went to. The televisions on the walls played sports, though one was set to something that looked like MTV. Michael led him to a table where two people sat—a slender, somewhat effeminate dark-haired guy and a blond man who must have been six foot three.

The darker of the two stood slightly as he saw them approach, and waved to Michael. "Hey, honey! Glad to see you came up for air."

Nicky wondered what the guy meant by that, but he was hit with a rush of understanding. The guy was talking about sex. Specifically, the sex Michael and Nicky were having. Bile rose in Nicky's throat.

"Guys, this is Nicky." Michael jutted his nose in the air, clearly ignoring his friend's comment.

"Nicky, this is Henri..." Michael gestured at the dark-haired guy, who now that Nicky really looked at him did have French features. Namely, a longish nose and eyes dark enough to be black. "And Logan. Logan is a firefighter too."

The blond guy leaned across the table to hold out a hand for Nicky to shake. "I'm at the 25. Not sure we've met." He had a cute Southern accent that put Nicky at ease right away.

Gratefully, Nicky shook Logan's hand. "I'm down at the 13." He didn't think he'd ever spoken to Logan, but the guy was mildly familiar. Nicky had probably seen him before.

"Grab a seat." Henri scooted out of the booth, since he'd been sitting across from Logan, and gave Michael and Nicky the bench. "I'll get drinks. What do you guys want?"

Michael eased into the bench first, thankfully giving Nicky the outer seat. "We'll have beers," Michael ordered for the both of them. "See if they have a pilsner on tap."

Henri raised an eyebrow at Michael, calling him out for his pushiness.

"What?" Michael scrunched up his shoulders defensively. He turned to Nicky. "Did you want something different?"

Nicky smiled, but he rubbed his face to hide it. Something told him not to get on Henri's bad side. "No, it's fine. That'll be great, thanks." Between more packing, visiting his mother at All Saints, and now coming to his first gay bar ever, Nicky was far too overwhelmed to spend time thinking about what to order.

"See?" Michael gave his friend a haughty glare. "It's fine."

It was clear from the hand on his hip that Henri was unconvinced, but he flounced off to the bar.

When he came back a few minutes later, he'd managed to get a tray from the bar and carried over not only the beers Nicky and Michael had ordered, but also a round of shots.

"Henri's like this." Michael leaned into Nicky's side. "We can go for a walk after if we need to sober up before driving home."

Nicky smiled. He was glad Michael could see how Henri's behavior was a little over the top. Eyes stinging from the alcohol, Nicky joined Michael in downing their small amber shots.

Across the table from them, Henri sat next to Logan. Logan pressed a kiss onto Henri's mouth, and—seemingly in retaliation—Henri took a large swallow out of Logan's pint glass. Logan grabbed Henri's flank, and after a heated glance between them, they dove at each other's faces, playing tonsil hockey like a couple high school kids.

"Ahem!" Michael's throat clearing was obvious enough that Henri stopped what he was doing to glare.

"What?"

"We didn't come here for a live sex show." Michael moved his beer in front of him like he was building a wall between him and Henri.

"I don't mind," Nicky said under his breath. He'd have thought it would be weird, watching two men kiss in public. But Henri and Logan's display put Nicky at ease. At least no one would be staring at Nicky and Michael.

Henri tossed a coaster across the table like a Frisbee. It hit Michael's beer and ricocheted off. "You're always such a prude, chéri. Nicky must be quite a man to have gotten a piece of your clenched buttocks."

Nicky coughed mid-sip, sending droplets spraying across the table. "I... I don't..." He rushed to wipe the beer off his face, eyeing the table in vain for a napkin. "Shit. I'm sorry." Nicky couldn't handle looking up and seeing whether Logan and Henri had gotten wet, so he hopped up to borrow a bar towel.

He sighed out a few deep breaths, calming himself as he went to grab napkins out of the holder on the bar. When he turned, he saw that Logan had come over to meet him.

"Hey. Um, sorry if you got sprayed." Nicky held out a napkin.

"No worries." Logan wiped his hands. He gave Nicky a sympathetic smile. "You holding up okay?"

Nicky wasn't sure whether Logan was referring to the bar scene or whether Logan knew something about Nicky's mom.

"I guess." Nicky glanced over to their table where Michael and Henri looked like they were arguing, and decided not to rush to get back.

"Henri told me you're new to this." Logan jutted his chin in a gesture that meant "this gay bar thing". "I just moved to Seattle around Christmas, and I wasn't really out until a few months ago. It's a little weird at first."

"Nah. It's not too strange." Between working twenty-four-hour shifts, taking care of his mother nonstop, and now sleepovers with Michael, Nicky had lost his sense of normal. "It might be weird if I came alone, y'know, but with Michael..."

Everything he did with Michael was fun. Even packing and hauling things out of his mom's house. Nicky couldn't imagine trying to make a life for himself as a gay man without Michael being there for him.

"Oh, yeah. I imagine." Logan took another swig of his beer and gave a good-natured chuckle. "And Henri's been so cool. You know the first time I brought him to my place I hadn't come out to my roommates?" Logan's belly laugh made Nicky want to join in, even though his stomach started to squirm. "Thought Henri would tear me a new one over that. But he was good about it."

"I'm not out to my family," Nicky blurted, feeling like he had to confess to someone. Granted, his family was only his mom, but it felt like more than that. The guys at the station, Nicky didn't care about. He'd been the poor guy with the dying mom for so long that them finding out he was the poor guy who was gay probably wouldn't be a stretch. But it wasn't just his mom he was lying to. It was the folks at All Saints, and Father MacKenzie...

Nicky felt split into different pieces.

"That's okay." Logan shrugged. "Sometimes these things take a while."

"Yeah." Nicky gave a rueful laugh that came out more like a snarl. "I don't really have a while, though."

Logan tilted his head, his eyebrows lowering in question, but he didn't ask Nicky to clarify.

"It's just my mom, really. And she's..." He couldn't say she was *dying* to this guy he just met, as nice as Logan seemed.

"Oh, yeah. Henri told me." Logan gave Nicky that frown Nicky had gotten so used to. Sympathy and kindness, but packaged in a way that made it clear the person had no idea what to say.

"Yeah. No worries. I mean... Not like I'm over it. But I'm coming to terms with things." That morning, Nicky had scheduled a counseling session at All Saints—something they offered for families with dying relatives. He hadn't mentioned it to Michael. Nicky didn't know why, but he needed to work things out on his own before he could let Michael in.

"Well, that's good. For you," Logan stammered, but Nicky could tell he was trying. "But if it's just her that doesn't know, does it matter?" He flipped his hands palm up in a move of supplication. "Does she have to?"

Nicky glanced away, scanning the bar for Michael and Henri.

"It's none of my business."

"No. It's okay." Of course, Nicky had considered Logan's perspective. Over and over. Hell, his mom barely remembered things Nicky told her from day to day. In all likelihood if he told her he was gay, it wouldn't even register.

He still felt a dark place in his heart though, like there was this huge part of himself he couldn't share with her and who she'd never know because he was too scared.

"Hey there, guys." Henri came bounding up, followed by Michael, and climbed onto a barstool next to Logan. "What have you handsome fellows been talking about?"

Logan smirked. "You, baby. All about you."

Henri beamed.

Nicky wished he could come up with something that snarky to say to Michael, but since his mind was full of whether or not he needed to come clean with his mother, he buried his face in Michael's neck instead, breathing in the smell of comfort and happiness, and trying to forget all his questions.

Chapter Fourteen

Nicky had been preoccupied all night, and Michael was glad when Nicky agreed to come to Michael's apartment to sleep. He needed to do laundry, and cook in his own kitchen. Not to mention, Nicky's house was still in flux—with boxes and dust and stuff that needed packing.

All the windows in the studio apartment were open, letting in the cool night air, and the street noise outside was louder than it had been all summer since kids were coming back to school.

They undressed silently, and Nicky got into bed first, his face knit with worry.

"You okay?" Michael turned off the bedside lamp and climbed in after him. Resting his hand on Nicky's shoulder, he urged Nicky closer. "You're fine with having gone out, right?"

"Yeah." Nicky sounded distracted. "Your friends are nice."

Michael nodded, snuggling into Nicky's side. He didn't expect they'd get off together that night, but Michael still liked being close. "Yeah. Too bad Jesse and Tomas couldn't make it. They live down in the south end and can be lazy about driving into town sometimes."

Nicky shifted so he was partway facing Michael. "I'd been meaning to talk to you about something..."

"Yeah?"

"About my mom. And her not knowing..."

"Uh-huh?" Michael cared less about Nicky's mom knowing than about the other people at the hospice center. The problem was—Nicky couldn't tell the staff he and Michael were together if he didn't tell his mother. Michael had always assumed coming out of the closet was simple, and that it would happen all at one time. Man, he'd been wrong. "Your mom seemed really nice when I met her. Maybe she won't react the way you're expecting."

"I don't think I can tell her." Nicky hung his head, like he was tired and wrung out and so exhausted by his mother's battle that he had nothing left to give.

Michael resigned to be empathetic and to put his own needs and desires aside. "I'll cope, okay?" Michael rubbed Nicky's shoulder. "You don't have to tell her just for me."

"Maybe I wouldn't be doing it just for you." Nicky's eyes shone in the darkened light of the room. "Sometimes I think... Maybe if I'd talked to her about it sooner..."

Michael slid his calf over Nicky's, wishing he could massage out Nicky's stress. "I know. And I wish I could know her better and that we could all hang out for Thanksgiving or Christmas. But..." Michael paused, not knowing if he should say what was on his mind. "I don't think that's in the cards."

Nicky tugged away. "She'll still be around for my birthday in November."

"I bet she will be." Michael was in no position to argue, but he suspected that even if Nicky's mother was still in this world then, she wouldn't be in great shape to celebrate.

"I wish you had time to know each other. I think she really would like you." Nicky's voice was so sad. All Michael could do was hold Nicky until his body relaxed and he slipped away into sleep.

Michael shut off the car and got out. His mom wasn't out front for once, and he didn't find her until he wandered all the way to the backyard. She was bent over some ferns, digging mulch into the ground.

In a rush, he realized that no matter how much she pissed him off and drove him crazy, he loved her.

He'd told her right away when he'd realized he liked boys, and practically the next day she went to his school to talk to his teachers about equality and rights, and to demand they make sure Michael was never teased for his orientation.

Maybe she'd jumped the gun—Michael had been horribly embarrassed at the time—but she'd cleared the way for him to be the man he was now.

"Hey, Mom."

"Oh, sweet goddess!" His mom flinched, hand crossing over her heart. "You scared the shit out of me."

Michael shrugged, the sadness that had been dogging him since talking to Nicky about Lydia tugging at his guts. "Sorry. Didn't mean to."

"That's okay." She pulled off her gardening gloves and smoothed down her skirt. "To what do I owe the honor of this unannounced visit?" She smiled at him, grinning at her joke, but slowly her face went slack with a frown. "Is something wrong?"

Michael couldn't believe he'd come here of all places for advice. His mom was always shoving unsolicited words of wisdom down his throat. But sadly, he couldn't think of anyone else to go to. "Yeah. I guess." Another shrug. Maybe he should man up and start from the beginning. "It's just that I'm dating someone now, and he's going through some rough stuff. And I'm not sure how to help." Michael nibbled the edge of his fingernail, something he'd thought he'd gotten over as a kid. "And I don't know what's right, y'know? What to expect. I don't know if I should give him space, or push to be closer. We spend a lot of time together…"

His mother's gaze was piercing. "How long have you been seeing him?"

He didn't know whether to count those first few weeks as dating, or even include the very first time they'd hooked up. "A month-ish." Michael rolled his eyes. "But could you please not be annoyed I didn't tell you sooner?"

There was a quirk in his mother's lips that said she would hold back her commentary for another time. "Okay, fine. But what's his problem?"

Michael took a shuddering breath, as the enormity of what Nicky was going through washed over him. "Do you remember when Grandma Elba died?"

His mom nodded, her face serious. Elba had been Michael's father's grandma.

"Well, he's going through something like that. But with his mom."

Without a word, his mother opened her arms. And though Michael tensed at what was coming next, he let it happen. Weird as it always was to get crushed into his mother's generous bosom, he realized that if he were in Nicky's position, he'd never get a chance to feel that awkwardness. That mixture of disgust and need and even love. He wouldn't have his mom to be annoyed at anymore.

"Let's go have some tea." His mother patted his arm and urged him in the back door to her breakfast nook. "We'll talk about your man."

"Are you sure you're up for this?" Michael stood at Nicky's side, though Michael stayed two feet away like they were friends instead of lovers.

"I guess." Nicky spared a moment to look down the block at the Mustang, which Michael had finally picked up from the shop. The paint was still rusted off in places, but it ran again.

Nicky was so glad Michael had opted to repair it instead of selling it for parts. Old things were worth keeping, taking care of, fixing. Silly that Nicky found Michael's attachment to his car endearing, but it was one of the reasons he loved Michael so much.

"Are we going to go in, then?" Michael smirked, nodding at the front of the bar. Though it was still light outside, the bar's windows were filled with beer ads and signs. Nicky's firefighting buddies inside probably couldn't see him and Michael, but Nicky still wondered if Cody and the guys were staring.

"Yeah." Before he could lose his nerve, Nicky reached out and grabbed Michael's hand. "I love you," he blurted. Nicky's stomach was filled with butterflies. "And it's okay if you don't feel that way about me yet...or at all. I know shit with you is—"

Michael cut him off with a kiss. And even though Nicky's pals might have been able to see, Nicky relaxed and let Michael do it. Michael's whiskers were soft, and he tasted like mouthwash. He tasted perfect.

"I love you too, dummy." Michael set Nicky back, wide mouth smirking and blue eyes dancing in the evening light.

"You think I go to this kind of trouble with every guy I blow in a park?"

Nicky grinned so hard he must have looked like an idiot. The big, shining bubble of happiness inside him carried him through the door and into the darkened bar, hand in hand with his boyfriend.

The guys were in the back, at their normal seats by the pool table. Usually, Nicky didn't think twice about his friends' hangout, but now that he was with Michael, Nicky realized the place smelled distinctly like spilled, stale beer and the carpet was not just worn down, but also sticky.

None of his pals looked up until Nicky and Michael had made it halfway across the room. Cody glanced over, and he gave Nicky a smile and a wave, before doing a double take at the way Nicky and Michael were holding hands.

On reflex, Nicky tried to shake off Michael's hold, but Michael gripped him all the harder.

"It'll be fine," Michael murmured low enough that only Nicky would hear over the classic-rock soundtrack.

Nicky was glad as hell Michael hadn't let go. If Nicky backed out now, he'd regret it.

"Hey." Nicky nodded at Cody, and at the new guy Ralph who sat next to him. Nicky's boss, Hank, was a few seats down, and he lifted an eyebrow at Nicky and Michael showing up together, but blinked a few times, as if to erase the expression of surprise from his face.

"Hey." Cody slapped Nicky's hand in greeting, his eyes on Michael the whole time. "Glad you could make it out. How's your mom doing?"

Nicky knew his friend was just asking the same question the guys at the station always felt the need to ask, but tonight Nicky didn't want to answer. For once, he wanted to talk to his friends about the good news in his life instead of the bad. "She's okay." Nicky cleared his throat. "I, uh, wanted you guys to meet Michael. He's my..." Nicky could feel his heartbeat in his ears, and his vision tunneled so that all he could focus on was the reaction he was expecting on Cody's face. "Michael's my boyfriend."

"Oh." Cody made this move with his neck and shoulders, like a nod, but with a forward bouncing of his whole body. "Oh, well, uh, good to meet you." Cody jerked his hand upwards, like maybe he'd go for a handshake, but Michael headed him off with a wave instead.

"Yeah, hi. You're Cody, right? Nicky's mentioned you." Michael's ramrod posture was the same as always, and if anything, it made Cody's awkward bobbing and weaving seem almost apologetic.

"Yeah, uh. You meet the rest of the guys yet?" Cody twisted to make more introductions, appearing happy to have something to do other than stare openmouthed at Nicky and Michael.

All the other guys—even Hank, who was old enough Nicky expected him to say something mean—acted pretty much the same as Cody. Each and every one of them waved or shook hands casually, like they met coworkers' same-sex partners every day of the week.

Nicky knew they were faking it and were more freaked out than they let on. But over the years he'd learned how to spot when people just didn't know what to say.

His pals might have felt awkward. Or confused. But they were trying. And Nicky appreciated their effort.

"So, do you want me to grab us some beers?" Michael knocked Nicky's side, but thank God he didn't do anything as familiar as throwing his arm around Nicky's shoulder. Nicky had learned that Michael was actually pretty reserved about public displays of affection. One more thing that made Nicky love the guy.

"Yeah." Nicky smiled, hoping he wasn't grinning like a freak at his boyfriend. "Grab me a pilsner?"

He could tell Michael wanted to kiss him, but Michael pressed his lips together instead. "Sure thing."

Chapter Fifteen

"How are you doing today?" Nicky settled into the seat next to his mother's bed. Her hand lay across the side rail, draped like she'd fallen asleep in an odd position. He picked it up to make sure she didn't lose circulation and rubbed it between his hands. "Getting a good sleep?"

Nicky was glad Michael had gone back to school and stopped asking to come visit Nicky's mother with him because Nicky was running out of excuses to keep Michael away. Each and every time Nicky sat here in this same seat, he thought of the words he wanted to come out of his mouth. But even when his mom was sleeping, like she did most of the time now, he couldn't seem to form the sentences. Where to start? When he was eleven, hiding in his room staring at muscle and fitness magazines, trying to figure out what it was about them that made them so fascinating? When he'd been thirteen and rushing to wash his sheets so his mom and dad wouldn't find out what had happened in his bed at night?

His mother had grown up Catholic, but she'd tried to be as open as she could with him about sex. Nicky recalled those awkward, nerve-wracking conversations in the car when she'd tried to talk to him about "changes" and how they were "normal". Yet Nicky had known, already in those earliest days, the changes he was going through weren't normal. At least not all of them. But he'd known his mother was trying so hard. He hadn't wanted to push her any further.

"Nicky?" She lolled her head to the side, her eyes only opening for a second as she struggled to focus. "Why aren't you at school?"

Nicky pinched his lips together, focusing on the good. She was awake and remembered his name. He'd worried that after the stroke she'd had a few days ago she wouldn't be able to recall that much.

"It's a holiday, Mom." He bent to rub his cheek against her hand. The skin was soft, less dry than it used to be, maybe because her kidneys were failing and she'd started retaining water. "It's a holiday, so I had a day off."

"Good." Her eyes crinkled in the corners, like she wanted to smile even though the rest of her face had forgotten how. "Good. You play."

"Mom..." He knew she wouldn't understand him. Wouldn't remember. But fuck, he had to tell her now, while she was still conscious and had some chance of knowing. "You remember my friend? Michael? He came to the house?"

He searched her face for some kind of comprehension, some glimmer that the day he and Michael had moved her still existed in her mind.

"The house?" She blinked, her eyes landing on the space around her. "Where...?" Her forehead creased like she was both confused and upset. "Where am I?"

Nicky reached for the remote control and flicked to one of the stations she liked. It was airing an old episode of *Friends* that they'd watched together a hundred times. "Look. It's the one where Joey teaches Chandler how to do nothing all day."

His mom let out a breath, raspy and thick, but more relaxed. "Oh." She looked in the direction of the sound from the TV, though Nicky was fairly certain she couldn't see it.

She calmed, distracted from everything around her. Nicky finally admitted to himself—he wasn't going to tell her. Not today. Not ever. His opportunity had passed awhile ago. Maybe before he even met Michael. He licked his lips, tasting the salty tears that had gathered on his stubble.

"I'm coming with you, and that's final." Michael grabbed the shirt that Nicky had been holding and tossed it in the laundry basket. Nicky was a mess. Understandable since they'd just gotten a call from All Saints that Nicky's mother had experienced another stroke—this one fatal—but Michael still wasn't going to let Nicky head out with coffee spilled across his chest.

Fatal...the word echoed in Michael's consciousness, thrummed in his body. But he couldn't get swept away in thinking about what it all meant. He needed a clear head for Nicky.

"But...I don't think..." Nicky stared around their bedroom, like he was looking for the T-shirt Michael had taken, or a replacement, and couldn't imagine where to find it.

Michael dragged open Nicky's drawers and pulled out some clothes for him. They had more space now that they'd moved into Lydia's old bedroom, but the house still felt cramped since Michael had moved all his things in when he'd found someone to take over his lease in the U District.

"You're not safe to drive." Michael urged the T-shirt over Nicky's head. "If you want me to stay in the parking lot, I will. But I'm taking you there, and there's no point in arguing."

When the T-shirt had cleared Nicky's chin, Michael could see that Nicky was crying. Michael wanted to hold Nicky, but if Michael did that, he would start crying too, and they'd never manage to get to All Saints without an accident.

"Come on. Get dressed." Michael reached for his own pants, finding that his hands were shaking. Even after the months he and Nicky had been together, he'd only met Lydia the one time. Still, Michael felt like he knew her. He saw her influence in how Nicky kept his house clean, or the way he'd make the sign of the cross when he hoped a sports team he liked would score.

"I can't believe…" Nicky stood there in his briefs, jeans dangling from his hand. "I should have been there."

"No." Michael took the pants out of Nicky's hand and bent to a crouch to get them on Nicky's legs. Stupid, maybe, to dress him like he was a kid, but Michael knew Nicky needed to be taken care of, and unlike the past months when Michael had seen Nicky miserable and not known what to do, now, today, he could take charge and fix things. "There was no way you could have known to be there."

At least Nicky had the presence of mind to do up his fly on his own. When he was done, he looked at Michael like he had no idea where he was or what he was doing.

"Come on." Michael took his hand. There wasn't any time crunch, really. The folks at All Saints had said not to hurry. But Michael knew Nicky needed to get there, to be by his mother's side, even if she could no longer see him.

Nicky followed down the stairs and into Michael's Mustang. Trying to make his brain work, Michael ran through whether they'd left on the stove or if any doors were unlocked. He made sure to watch behind him as he backed out of Nicky's driveway, especially since some parts of the road were still slick with fallen leaves.

"I'm supposed to go to work in an hour." Nicky stared out the windshield as he said it, his face full of awe and panic.

Michael checked the clock on the car's dash and saw that it was seven fifteen.

If Nicky hadn't been awake and getting ready for work, they would have been asleep when All Saints called. "I'll contact Hank, okay?" Michael rubbed Nicky's thigh, feeling nothing but tense muscle under his jeans.

"Okay."

"It'll be okay." He squeezed Nicky's hand as hard as he dared. "We'll take care of everything." The will, the funeral arrangements—all that Michael could handle, but he had no idea what to say to make Nicky feel any better.

He could have used some flowery words about how Nicky's mother wasn't in pain anymore, or that she'd be in a better place, or even that they'd known this was coming for a while. But if Michael's mother had died, he would smack anyone who tried to tell him how to feel.

"I know." Nicky gripped Michael's hand, like it was all Nicky could do to tread water. "I know you will. And, fuck, I... God, I love you so much."

Michael lifted their hands and kissed Nicky's knuckles. "I know, baby." He held Nicky's hand until he parked at the hospice center.

"Here we are." Michael got out of the car, wondering if he should go inside with Nicky. "You want me to come with you?"

As scattered as Nicky seemed, Michael needed to ask, because if Michael did the wrong thing today, he wasn't sure if he could live with himself.

"Um...yeah." Nicky got out of the car and started toward the hospice center.

Michael followed, opening the door for him when Nicky couldn't seem to remember how, and walking at his side as Nicky went to the front desk.

"Hi there, Nicky." The receptionist gave Nicky a sympathetic smile.

Of course she knew him. Nicky had been coming here every day he wasn't working for months.

"Where is she?" Nicky swallowed, eyes lost. Michael would have put his arm around Nicky's shoulders, except he wasn't sure what Nicky was comfortable with.

"In her room." The woman glanced past Nicky to Michael. "Does your friend need a visitor's pass?"

Nicky blinked like he didn't know what she was asking, but then he swung around to look at Michael. The longing and fear and need was written all over Nicky's face, and if Michael could have right then, he would have pulled Nicky close so Nicky didn't have to struggle with his feelings alone.

"Yeah." Nicky reached for Michael's hand. He caught it in his own and pulled Michael a step closer. "Yeah, could he have a visitor's pass?"

The nurse, or whoever the lady was wearing pink scrubs, lifted her cheeks in the closest thing to a smile that could be expected on a day like today. She pushed the clipboard Michael's direction. "Under 'relationship', put 'partner'. It'll make things easier if you need to help Nicky through paperwork later."

Michael nodded but kept his attention down. He hoped Nicky was okay with that nomenclature, because Michael would do whatever made things smoother for Nicky. "Thanks." He scribbled his name, and the time, and "partner" in that place where all things were decided about who was what to whom, and he handed the clipboard back to the woman.

"You can go on to her room now." The woman glanced down the hall in the direction Michael had taken with Nicky over two months ago. How different things had been then—heady, but rushed, the way they'd been with Mark when Michael was so high on emotion he'd never thought to look down and see that there was nothing holding up their relationship.

Now, as he held Nicky's hand down the long walk to Nicky's mother's room, everything was different. The longing was there, and the love and even the excitement, but the foundation between them was broad and strong. Firm, like the cornerstone of a building.

The door to Nicky's mother's room was closed, and a priest stood next to it. For a second, Michael had a strange sense of déjà vu, wondering where he'd seen the guy before. But then Nicky's hand tightened on Michael's and Michael remembered.

It was the guy who'd been at Nicky's house back in August.

"Nicolas." The priest stared at the two of them with stern eyes, his attention traveling from their faces to their joined hands.

Michael loosened his grip. He didn't need a showdown. Not now of all times, and certainly not with a man he and Nicky might never see again.

"Father." Nicky gripped Michael's hand all the harder, like he'd strangle Michael's fingers before letting go.

"You're not planning to go in there like that, are you?" The priest glared as if they were committing some kind of wrong just for showing up together.

"Listen." Michael hated to get in the middle of this, but fuck if he would let this man make Nicky feel worse. "You don't have any right—"

Nicky tugged Michael's arm, soft but sure enough that Michael shut his mouth.

"While I've appreciated everything you've done for my mom..." Nicky took a deep breath, rubbing his jaw with the hand that wasn't gripping Michael's. "I don't think you understand—"

"Oh, I understand perfectly well." The way the priest narrowed his eyes was crueler than anything Michael would have expected.

Sheltered as Michael had been in his mom's liberal bubble, he wasn't sure he'd ever seen such blind hatred in a person's gaze. It forced him back a step, made him want to shake his hand away from Nicky's and play it cool until he and Nicky were somewhere else.

"What do you understand?" Nicky advanced on the priest, meeting scorn with outrage. "That Michael is my boyfriend? That we're together? Lovers? Partners?"

Michael held Nicky back, because the way Nicky's hands were fisted bordered on frightening.

"Your mother never would have approved." The priest blustered, wiping his forehead, but he retreated until he hit the pale blue wall behind him.

"You have no idea what my mother would have thought." Nicky leaned toward the priest, like he was fighting Michael's grip, but just enough to make sure Michael still had a firm hold on his biceps. "And now neither one of us will know. But I do know this—my mom loved me." The pain in Nicky's face was hard to watch because it made his handsome features twist into a mask of pure sadness. "And she would have wanted to know me... If she'd lived, she would have wanted..." His voice cracked, broke. Nicky's shoulders shook hard enough that Michael wrapped his arms around him to hold him lest Nicky's emotions spill out and tear him apart. "She would have wanted to know me."

Nicky twisted to let Michael take some of his weight. Michael couldn't bear to look at Father MacKenzie. And there was nothing he could think of to say. So he closed his eyes and buried his face in Nicky's hair, rubbing his back while listening to the footsteps that meant the priest had finally stormed off.

"She would have still loved me," Nicky murmured into the crook of Michael's neck.

For the first time since they'd gotten that phone call, Michael knew the right thing to say. "Yeah, she would have, Nicky. She would have told you she loved you no matter what, and that she'd always be your mom."

The words came easy to Michael because he still remembered the things his own mother had said. At the time, they'd seemed almost canned. Maybe trite. He'd been raised with the notion that people of all races and sexes and orientations were equal and had been treated to speeches on it every few days at dinner.

Now Michael understood why people used the phrase "count your blessings". Sometimes a person didn't know all the ways they'd been lucky until they saw someone who wasn't. "She and I would have been great friends." Michael continued his soft words, rubbing Nicky's back as they stood outside his mother's door.

He said them over and over until Nicky loosened his hold on Michael's shirt.

Wiping his face, Nicky pulled away. He glanced down the hall like he was worried someone had seen him crying. Funny, because what in the hell else was a guy supposed to do when he'd found out his mother was gone?

"I guess I should go in."

Michael rubbed Nicky's arm. "You want me to go with you?"

"No." Nicky stood up taller. He sighed, seeming to lose most of the panic he'd been harboring all morning. "No, I want to go in alone."

"Okay." Michael stepped back, and with one last squeeze and caress of Nicky's arm, let go. "I'll be right here when you're done."

Nicky took his mother's hand. She looked almost the same as before, though all the machines that used to buzz around her were turned off and stowed, leaving the room eerily quiet.

If there was a little more coolness to her skin, and more rigidity to her tissues, Nicky ignored it as he sat at her side like he'd done every day he'd had off since August.

"Hey, Mommy." He rubbed a thumb across her knuckles, thinking that somehow she could still hear him. "I...I want to tell you something..."

The image of her hand blurred as his eyes filled with wetness. Nicky waited for the tears to drop. "You know that friend of mine you met? Michael?" He shook his head because he could almost imagine her butting in and saying something that would stop him from getting it out. "Well, he's not really my friend."

He'd said the words so many times, it was funny how hard it was to say them to her. "I love him. I'm in love with him."

Even though he knew there was no way she could answer, Nicky waited. He sat there, wondering how she would respond. Trying to figure out something she might have said to set him at ease and help him make it through tomorrow and the day after and the day after that.

"So I'm gay," he pushed. Still no answer. Of course there wouldn't be, but fuck it, he wished there was one. "I have been for years, I guess. Forever." Anger made his voice tremble, and he didn't know where it came from. Maybe it didn't matter. "I should have told you." She might have been furious. Or sad. Hell, it was possible she would have thrown a fit and kicked him out in the street. But Nicky didn't think she would have. "I wish I'd told you."

He nodded, paused. "I'm sorry I didn't tell you."

In his mind's eye, he imagined his mom touching the top of his head the same way she had when he was sick or scared or had a nightmare as a little boy and couldn't sleep. Nicky knew it was imagination, and possibly wishful thinking. But it was the only answer he was going to get.

Now that she was gone he had to choose his own answers. As much as Nicky wanted to punish himself with harsh ones, he chose to believe the ones Michael gave him. That the world was filled with good people, or at least people who were trying. And no one cared one way or another if you were gay.

"I'll miss you, Mommy." Nicky pressed his lips together so he wouldn't lose it entirely. He rose and kissed his mom's forehead. "I'll miss you so much."

Nicky spun away, unable to do this any longer, and yet knowing he'd replay it over and over in his head.

Leaving his mom behind, he pushed open the door and stepped into the hallway where Michael was leaning against the wall.

"You okay?" Michael's expression was so serious. Forehead creased, frown digging into his short beard. Blue, Norwegian eyes concerned and stable and everything Nicky needed.

"Yeah." Nicky grabbed Michael's arm. He couldn't curl back into Michael's side now. He had to plan the details of his mom's burial and funeral and everything else. No way in hell was he doing the service at Father MacKenzie's church. "Let's go deal with the paperwork."

Chapter Sixteen

Michael's dress pants were a size too small, since his mom had bought them for him to wear to a cousin's wedding years ago. He held a bible in front of his crotch so he could pick at the fabric digging into his balls.

Hopefully people didn't get sent to hell for thinking about their nuts in church.

"Thank God Father Walters could work this out on such short notice." Nicky shuffled farther into the bench, taking Michael's hand to lead him deeper. A handful of firefighters Michael recognized from Nicky's battalion filed in next to them, each nodding his condolences to Nicky.

In the bench in front of them, Henri and Logan stood next to Tomas and Jesse. Jesse twisted to give Nicky a sympathetic smile.

"Hey. Um, I'm sorry for your loss." Jesse and Nicky had only met a couple times, but Michael was so glad his friend had agreed to attend.

"Thanks." Nicky gripped Jesse's hand, and some unspoken emotion passed between them.

Michael wrapped his arm around Nicky's shoulder and gave him a squeeze.

The church was decked with white garlands, and candles lit every wall. At the front, an enormous, gilded cross hung suspended over the pulpit. The place had a funny smell, more complex than the Nag Champa guys had burned in dorm rooms to cover the scent of weed. It smelled more like the smudge sticks his mother had used sometimes when she decided to try on some religion for a few months. Not unpleasant, just...maybe memorable was the right word.

Michael looked over his shoulder, wondering what the chances were his mother would decide to show up at the last minute. Between school starting and everything with Nicky's mother, Michael hadn't had the chance to bring Nicky home to meet her yet. But he had invited her to the ceremony.

In a flutter of shawls, his mom came bustling in and shuffled her way into the backmost pew. Seeing Michael, she waved, smiling.

He smiled back. "Hey." Michael touched Nicky's sleeve. "My mom showed up." He jerked his head toward the back of the room.

Nicky turned, squinting. When he figured out which woman was Michael's mother, his face cracked into a wide smile. "You have her nose."

Michael rolled his eyes. For some reason, he'd never liked being compared to her.

The organ kicked up, and everyone turned to watch a procession of the priest and some other guys who flanked him. They all wore white with gold sewn into the seams, and Michael had to admit that the spectacle was pretty. Or maybe it was something else. Maybe *moving* was the right word. But Michael didn't know if he wanted to be moved. In fact, he was pretty sure he didn't. It was only when he looked to Nicky and saw the joy in his eyes that Michael knew what he'd come here for. To

195

be moved the way Nicky was, to be together with Nicky through thick and thin.

The priest got to the front of the room and stood on stage. "In the name of the Father, and the Son, and the Holy Spirit."

All at once, like a booming cannon, the people around answered, "Amen."

Michael panicked that he had no idea what he was supposed to be doing, so he checked Nicky for direction. Nicky's face was serene, and he pointed to the pamphlets people were holding. Copies lined the shelves behind the pews.

Michael grabbed a folded program out of the holder and checked for directions. Turned out the prayers were right there. Not wanting to look like an idiot, Michael answered along with Nicky and a hundred other people the next time the priest said his lines.

The rest of the mass went easily enough, and though Michael tensed at the mention of God delivering the congregation from evil—in case the evil they were talking about was his kind of evil—most of the service seemed to involve either singing or talking about Lydia.

After it was over, Nicky asked for a moment alone. Michael watched as he went to a quiet corner of the church where there was a wall of votive candles in small red cups. Nicky lit one, slipped a dollar in the slot next to the stand, and lowered onto his knees to clasp his hands in prayer.

Despite all the songs and the incense and the broad and hopeful words during the mass, none of it moved him like Michael was moved now. By the time Nicky got back, it was Michael who was wiping his face free of wetness, while Nicky's eyes were dry.

"You ready to go?"

Michael nodded. "Yeah." He didn't feel right taking Nicky's hand, so he just followed Nicky outside. Nicky's battalion were all lined up to shake his hand, and most of them shook Michael's hand immediately after without any of the nervous twitches Michael had seen when he'd first been introduced to Nicky's friends.

Michael's friends stood at the bottom of the steps, and when Nicky and Michael reached them, Henri pulled Nicky into a hug. Despite the seriousness of the day, Michael couldn't help but chuckle at Nicky's blush, especially when Henri grabbed Nicky's face and kissed both his cheeks.

"We're all thinking about you, chéri." Henri rubbed Nicky's arm.

Michael led Nicky away before Nicky had a chance to get any more embarrassed. "Thanks for coming." Michael shook hands with Logan and Jesse, and then, a little more reluctantly, Tomas.

Tomas had always liked to give Michael a hard time, but today Tomas dragged Michael into a hug. A lot of things were unspoken in that gesture. Michael had no idea whether Tomas meant it as an apology of sorts, or whether he was trying to tell Michael "good job" for sticking with Nicky through all of this.

Unsettled by Tomas's outpouring of affection, Michael took a couple steps away. He patted his pocket. After all the people they'd shaken hands with that day, he and Nicky were bound to have picked up all manner of germs. Plus, they were heading into cold-and-flu season. Taking out a bottle of hand sanitizer, he handed it to Nicky, before taking a dollop for himself.

"You almost ready to go?" Nicky leaned into Michael's side, rubbing his arm. They'd be heading to a reception after this, and still had a long day to go until they could collapse together at home.

"Yeah." Michael looked across the parking lot to where he remembered parking his Mustang and saw his mom making her way to their old family Subaru. "Hey." He grabbed Nicky's hand and urged him in her direction.

His mom turned as they approached. She wore a homemade cloak thing over her shawls, and though her clothes were a riot of fall colors as opposed to the black worn by the rest of the funeral-goers, her hair was brushed, and free of twigs and leaves. "Hi, Michael." She gave Nicky a smile. "You must be the boyfriend I've heard so much about."

Nicky nodded. His eyes were haunted, and Michael remembered why he hadn't wanted to introduce Nicky to his mother quite yet. Michael hadn't wanted to make Nicky miss his own mom more than he already did.

"I'm Eline." She touched Nicky's arm, and before Nicky could respond, she'd pulled him into an embrace. "I'm so sorry for your loss, honey." If Nicky had been blushing when Henri embraced him, it was nothing compared to the crimson color on Nicky's face now.

Michael tried not to smile, glad that they were in the parking lot, not right in front of the church where Nicky's buddies might have witnessed his embarrassment.

"Nice to meet you." Nicky disengaged himself. "I'm Nicky. Nicky O'Brian. Thanks for coming. I really appreciate it."

Michael's mother gave him a sympathetic smile. "I wouldn't have missed it." She lifted her hand, like she'd yank him into a hug again, but then lowered it to her side. "Michael's told me you have a birthday coming up. You should come around. I'll bake a cake."

"Sure thing." It was clear from the clouds in Nicky's eyes that Nicky was ready to get out of there, to spend time just the two of them before the next step in their day.

"We should get going, Mom." Michael leaned in to kiss her, making sure to keep a firm grip on her arm so he wouldn't get dragged into a hug himself.

"See you soon, boys." She waved as they left, then turned to open her car and climb inside.

When Michael reached the Mustang, he opened Nicky's door first. Holding it, he watched Nicky closely, wondering about Nicky's first impression of Eline.

"She can be a little enthusiastic. But she means well."

Nicky looked confused, or maybe disturbed, and he paused a second in the bend of the car door. "I don't think she was wearing a bra."

Despite the way the darker fall months had paled Nicky's skin, there was still a blush on his cheeks, contrasting with the somber black of his suit.

"Yeah." Michael gave Nicky's hand a reassuring squeeze. "She never does."

"Oh my God, Mom. What have you done?" Michael's mouth dropped open in a scowl.

Nicky rubbed his face to hide his chuckles. He'd gotten used to the way Michael and his mother bickered, and the look on Michael's face as he ogled his mother's cake was too funny not to laugh.

"I said white cake with chocolate icing. Why didn't you let me bring one over?" Michael swept his hand at his mother's kitchen island, at the cake she had made from scratch and the gloppy-looking brown stuff she was using for icing.

"I don't mind." Nicky tugged at Michael's arm. After all, they'd be getting together with Cody and a few guys from the station on Thursday. The party at Michael's mom's was a low-key thing, with Henri, Logan, Jesse and Tomas. As far as Nicky was concerned, Michael's mother could make any kind of cake she wanted.

"Well, you didn't expect me to make something out of a box, did you?" She picked up a glass jar labeled *gluten-free blend*, and opened her cabinet to put it on a shelf.

"Yes, Mom. I did expect you to make box cake—since I specifically asked for box cake." Michael had already gotten out a rag and was trying to wipe down the table as his mother did her best to get in the way. "And is the icing real chocolate, or did you use carob?" He reached to get a finger full, but his mother slapped his hand away.

"You won't be able to tell the difference." She tossed her head back indignantly, slightly pink nose in the air.

No way was Nicky getting in the middle of this argument. "I'm going to go talk to the guys." He gave Eline's arm a squeeze as he passed. "Thanks for doing this. I really appreciate it."

Eline's smile was more than a little smug, and Nicky had a feeling he'd catch hell later for siding with her—however remotely—over his boyfriend.

"You're very welcome." The passive-aggressive way she aimed the words at Michael were straight out of her son's playbook. Nicky had to get out of there before he let out a guffaw.

Despite the gloomy weather outside and the rain that had been pouring nonstop all week, Eline's house was a riot of plants and color. Paintings lay against walls, like she'd decided where they'd go but hadn't gotten around to hanging them, and trees and bushes in planters were tucked into every corner.

Nicky's mom had never been as into gardening as Michael's, but Nicky knew that some plants were supposed to be brought inside in winter. It seemed like Michael's mother had taken that edict to heart, hauling in the less-hearty stuff the way some people might bring in a pet from the yard.

"It's the birthday boy!" Henri sat nestled in an oversized chair, feet up on an ottoman while Logan perched on the armrest.

"Shut up." Nicky went to the couch and tried to figure out where to sit with Tomas and Jesse taking up most of it.

"Here." Tomas urged Jesse into his lap.

Jesse went in an awkward sprawl, blocking Tomas from view of the rest of the room.

"Thanks." Nicky dropped next to the guys. There was a pot of tea on the coffee table, and Nicky wrestled forward to pour himself a cup.

"So, is Michael getting you anything special for your birthday?" Tomas's muffled voice came from somewhere behind Jesse, but Nicky could still hear that he was being a smartass.

"Besides the blowjob this morning? I don't think so." Nicky said it quietly enough that Michael's mother wouldn't hear. Or more specifically, so Michael wouldn't hear. Nicky had a feeling Michael's mom wouldn't care.

"Well, I'm glad to hear our boy's treating you right." More muffled words from Tomas. His tough-guy routine would work better if he wasn't covered in five foot ten of floppy-haired twink.

"Jeez, Louise." Jesse twisted on Tomas's lap, though whether he managed to see Tomas's face Nicky couldn't tell. "It's not enough that you pick on Michael, you have to get on his boyfriend's case too? You know, we're not going to get invited anywhere if you keep this up."

Tomas must have started tickling Jesse at that point, because Jesse squirmed, giggling, but batting behind him at Tomas at the same time.

"Who's ready for cake?" Eline's voice rang out from the kitchen.

Michael walked ahead of her, rolling his eyes in frustration, but when he looked Nicky's direction, he was all smiles.

"We are! We are!" Henri bounded onto his knees in the chair.

"It's gluten-free," Michael grumbled, which Nicky found hilarious since practically everything Michael cooked didn't contain any wheat either.

"We won't hold that against the cake." Jesse gave Eline a wink.

She rounded the corner holding a cake that was lopsided and covered in candles that didn't match. Still, she'd managed to pair a three and a zero together to make a thirty, which was sweet. Scoops of ice cream lined the bottom, and Nicky was fairly certain they'd make a giant mess and have Michael bitching in no time.

"Haaaaaaaaappy birthday to you!"

Michael joined in with his mother, his voice rich, and Nicky couldn't believe he'd never heard Michael sing before because he was really good.

All the guys joined in, making Nicky want to hide his face. "Okay, okay!" He waved them to stop.

When he'd blown out the candles, everyone clapped and whooped, and Michael gave him a smile bright enough Nicky could almost forget the rain outside.

"I think I should cut this." Michael took charge of the knife, not giving his mom a chance to make a mess.

The cake was better than Nicky would have expected. Soft and chewy, though the icing wasn't particularly sweet. Still, with the homemade ice cream, the dessert was fantastic.

Jesse had to get to an evening class, so Michael and Nicky got out of there once everyone had finished the cake. They hurried through the rain to Michael's car, sliding into the seat so Michael could turn on the heat.

He rubbed his hands together, both to get rid of his frustration that his mother had screwed up Nicky's birthday cake, and to make sure his hands had proper circulation to drive.

Tomorrow, he'd make a cake at their place. The right kind. After all, he knew exactly what happened when he let other people be in charge.

"So where do you want to go?" Nicky asked, a small grin on his face.

"I don't know? Home?" Michael pulled away from the curb. He hadn't considered heading anywhere else since Nicky had work tomorrow and Michael had class in the morning.

"What, you don't want to go to a leather bar?" Nicky winked. "I'd think you'd want to rebel after the whole family-time thing."

Michael snickered. He and Nicky hadn't hung out with Michael's mother all that much, but apparently it had been enough for Nicky to sense that seeing his mom put Michael on edge. "Or we could just go home and play filthy choir boy."

Though Michael didn't have anything approaching a religious fetish, he'd become slightly obsessed with Nicky's stories of Catholic school.

Nicky on his knees. With his mouth open...waiting for the priest to put a wafer on his tongue...

Okay, seriously. Michael was really going to hell for thinking that, and he didn't even believe in God.

"I still have my uniform, you know." Nicky licked his lips. Oh yeah. He knew it got Michael off.

"I'm pretty sure you'd rip through the seams of it nowadays." Of course, Michael could get excited imagining that too. Maybe it was wrong and maybe it was slightly sick, but if Nicky wanted to play the Catholic schoolboy, Michael could get on board with that.

"You sound like you're complaining." Nicky took Michael's hand as they drove.

"No. I'm not." Hard as Michael was getting, this train of conversation was making Michael think of something he'd been mulling over for a while. "But, uh, there's something else I kinda want to..."

For years after Michael and Mark broke up, Michael hadn't really wanted to bottom. He'd felt so used and taken advantage of by Mark, and though on a logical level Michael knew there was nothing inherently demeaning about bottoming, he hadn't been able to fend off the notion that if he'd topped Mark, even once, he wouldn't have felt quite so miserable when they broke up.

"What?" Nicky's eyes lit up.

"Well, have you ever thought about...?" Michael couldn't believe how hard it was to say. His and Nicky's sex life had worked basically one direction since they'd been together. He worried Nicky would think less of him if he asked.

"Have I ever thought about what?" Nicky's lips twisted into a smirk, like he knew exactly what Michael was asking and just wanted to make Michael sweat.

Michael lifted his chin, unwilling to be made embarrassed. "I wondered if you might like to switch it up sometime." Michael didn't need it regularly. Hell, once a year would probably be enough. But he missed that feeling, a man against his back, on top of and in him. With how strong Nicky was, Michael could imagine—

"I'd do it if you want." Nicky leaned into Michael's side. His breath was quick on Michael's neck. "You'd like that, huh?"

Okay, not if Nicky was going to make fun of him. "No dirty talk. It's been a while for me..."

Nicky kissed his cheek. "Don't worry. I'll be gentle."

As it turned out, Nicky wasn't gentle at all.

About the Author

Retired party girl and '80s film enthusiast, Daisy Harris spends most of her time writing sexy romance and plotting the fall of Western civilization. Ms. Harris lives in Seattle, where she tortures her husband by making it rain. She enjoys watching bridges cause traffic, watching football games cause traffic and blithely wearing wool socks with sandals.

She has two little girls who've challenged Ms. Harris's feminist tendencies by insisting that makeup and high heels are appropriate for every occasion, including rock climbing and camping trips.

Daisy writes M/M romance about gods, zombies, firefighters and college boys. She's never missed an episode of *The Walking Dead*.

Find Daisy on Twitter as @thedaisyharris, on the web at

www.thedaisyharris.com

and on Tumblr at http://holsumcollege.tumblr.com.

They're going to need a bigger tent.

After the Rain
© *2014 Daisy Harris*
Fire and Rain, Book 2

Henri's list of bad exes is as long as his arm, but nothing prepared him for his latest, heart-stomping breakup. He thought he couldn't feel more abandoned, until his ride for a group camping trip bails, leaving him stuck driving for hours with a guy who is absolutely not his type.

After breaking up with his girlfriend of five years, firefighter Logan is working up the nerve to explore his interest in men. He knows he's gay. He just hasn't had the guts to do anything about it...until now.

Henri's big-city attitude and tight jeans push every last one of Logan's buttons, and when he and Henri have to share a tent, Logan is thrilled. He should have realized Pacific Northwest weather would get wet—forcing them to strip naked.

Though the steam between them is thicker than coastal fog, Henri's not sure he can let himself fall for another man. Not even the guy who finally treats him right.

Warning: Contains bad ex-boyfriends, even worse weather, and more than your average amount of sex in a tent. May not be suitable for those with germ phobias, outdoor aversions or fear of damp shoes.

Available now in ebook from Samhain Publishing.

SAMHAIN
PUBLISHING

It's all about the story...

Romance

HORROR

Retro
ROMANCE

www.samhainpublishing.com

CPSIA information can be obtained at www.ICGtesting.com
Printed in the USA
LVOW12s0513020615

440812LV00003BA/106/P